# The Enchanted Emerald

## By Donald Craghead

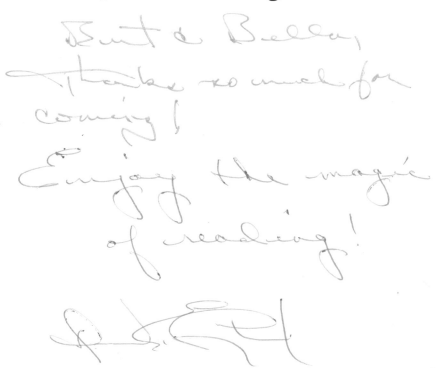

Burt & Bella,

Thanks so much for coming!

Enjoy the magic of reading!

TheEnchantedEmerald.com

# The Enchanted Emerald

## By Donald Craghead

October 2016
Monterey, California

This story is pure fiction, produced by a fertile and excited mind that has spent a lifetime reading and imagining. None of the character or events in this story are real. But that shouldn't stop the noble reader from thinking about what is possible.

# The Enchanted Emerald

ISBN-13: 978-1539386155

ISBN-10: 1539386155

Printed in the United States of America

# <u>Dedication</u>

To Jackie, who is everything.

and

To Isa, a future author.

*The Enchanted Emerald*

# *Acknowledgements*

The Enchanted Emerald would still be languishing on my computer where is sat for years if it was not for Margie McCurry and Tony Seton.

The story is short, the lead up to it quite long. Having written this book a number of years earlier and having it in the hands of an agent, I found the process of moving to the next stage of actually having the book published impossibly time-consuming and expensive. I finally requested the agent return the manuscript. Subsequently it remained on my computer for years until Margie McCurry took notice.

I posted a recent photo of myself on a social media website. Margie McCurry, a friendly acquaintance, noticed the photo and replied that it should be on the back of the book I should write. I messaged back to her that I had already written a book. Two weeks later Margie introduced me to Tony Seton of Seton Publishing. Three weeks after that I had a hard copy proof of The Enchanted Emerald in my hands. As a voracious reader myself, it was quite surreal after only reading this book on a computer screen to be holding an actual book in my hands.

My thanks to Margie McCurry for her tireless and proficient editing. My thanks to Tony Seton for getting this book into your hands!

*The Enchanted Emerald*

## CHAPTER 1

The old magician's stubby little legs were churning as fast as they could. The hem of his gray woolen robe was filthy with dust and weeds. He was too tired to hold it up from the ground. Old men were not meant to race down hillsides in terror, he thought.

"Hurry, Everett! I know you're tired, but I can hear him behind us!"

All the old man could do to answer his young apprentice's plea was make his puffing and panting louder as he ran. An occasional gasp punctuated his exertion.

They could hear the crashing brush and insane laughter as the assassin charged after them.

Croom was rushing down the hill from the castle that, as early as this morning, had been the magician's enclave. Since Croom had murdered all within, he now considered the castle to be the keep of the sole remaining young woman, Acantha. He continued his insane laughter as he pursued the last two magicians of the enclave. He chortled with glee as he imagined his rewards from Acantha upon completion of these last two murders. These two magicians – Michael, Acantha's brother, and Everett, the meddlesome old master magician that had taken the emerald ring from Acantha – would be the last to die.

"You can't outrun me!" shouted Croom. "Stop and die like men! Maybe I'll be nice enough to make it quick and painless."

Croom's crazed laughter rang through the trees as he ran and shouted at the two magicians. There was no question that when Croom finally ran his quarry to ground that he would easily be able to destroy them. He was a short man, less than five and one-half feet tall, but he was built like a bull. He had broad shoulders, a thick chest, and the limbs of a woodcutter.

Michael would do his best to defend himself and his beloved teacher from the butcher, but Michael was barely twenty, and had the slim, wiry build of a young man that was still filling out. Everett would be no help at all. He was a seventy year old man that was ready to collapse from exhaustion. The only reason that Croom had not caught up to them yet was that he wanted to play with them as a cat would play with a cornered mouse.

"No...more..." Everett managed to say between gasps for breath. He collapsed to the ground as he spoke. The hillside was thickly covered with overgrown brush and small trees. It was in a clearing from this heavy growth that Everett decided he could run no more.

"Take this," Everett said, as fatigue finally claimed him. "I can't go on. You must see to it that Croom does not get this ring. He will give it to Acantha and all will be lost."

Everett held out his hand. In his palm was a beautiful emerald of probably five carats, mounted in a massive gold setting.

"Come on, Everett, get up!" shouted Michael, as he nervously looked behind them. "Get up, you have to get up!"

He reached down to help the old man back to his feet. "No! No!" protested Everett, as he batted Michael's hands away. "Take this!" he insisted, as he thrust the ring into Michael's hands.

"Okay, okay, I have it," said Michael, as he quickly jammed it onto his finger. "Now, let's go."

"I can't outrun him and you know it," insisted Everett, as he weakly allowed Michael to pull him to his feet. "That's why I want you to take the ring. You can outrun him and keep the ring from Acantha."

"Forget it," snapped Michael. "We'll fight him together if we have to. Our magic will bring him down! At least yours will."

"Not possible, Michael. Acantha is using her magic through him. She has the ruby ring, and because of it her magic is stronger than the both of us. Don't allow her to get the emerald. She would rule the world if she had both rings. Run now while you....."

Croom ran screaming into the clearing, eyes glazed, mouth stretched wide, seemingly to the point of splitting open. Michael tried to block the rushing man's path to his beloved teacher, but the maddened murderer knocked him aside as he would a feather. Michael was still rolling in the sun-bleached grass and dirt when Croom crashed into the old man. Everett was knocked senseless with the collision and did not even have a chance to use his magical powers in an attempt to stop Croom.

Michael rose shakily from the ground as Croom stood staring at the fallen form of Michael's teacher. The powerfully-built man appeared enraptured at his deed, his face twisted into a rictus mask of viciousness. He bent to pick up a stout fallen limb from a nearby tree. Michael cried out in horror as he realized the stout limb was to be the tool used to end his friend's life.

Croom paused to look over at the terrorized boy. Then with a wicked smile, he raised the limb over his head to deliver the killing blow.

"NO!" screamed Michael. His sudden scream caused Croom to hesitate just a second, then the club began its wicked descent, slicing down toward Everett.

A vivid green light instantly enfolded Michael, focusing all of the power of his fear and impotent rage at seeing his old friend and teacher about to be destroyed by this madman. The light shot out from Michael and encompassed Croom in a swirling cyclonic force that threatened to pull the man apart.

Croom was twisted and pulled from his feet before the club struck Everett. He was hurled spinning into the same tree his weapon had fallen from, with force enough to break his back on impact. Face contorted with pain, the assassin felt his bones breaking, his organs bursting. Croom felt himself dying.

Michael sat in stunned silence watching the dust settle. He looked from Croom, to Everett, to the clearing around him.

Everett began to moan as he climbed his way back up to consciousness. He slowly and awkwardly brought himself to a sitting position.

"What happened?" he asked, as he looked around.

"I don't know," Michael responded. He held his hands up in a helpless gesture to show his own confusion. "I don't know," he repeated.

"Is that Croom?" The old man pointed at the crumpled heap under the tree.

Michael nodded. "Yeah. He came crashing into us, knocking us both to the ground. He was about to bash your brains in with that tree limb over there when there was this bright green flash of light. The next thing...."

"Green flash of light?"

"Yeah, I couldn't see anything after that for a minute or so. It sounded like someone was tearing these trees down, but I couldn't see what was happening because that flash blinded me. The next thing I know, you're coming to and Croom's a twisted heap."

"It worked! Thank God, it worked!"

"What do you mean, it worked? What worked?"

"The ring. The emerald ring." Everett groaned as he got to his feet. "God, I'm too old for this," he complained.

Michael quickly jumped to his feet with the ease of youth. He reached over to help Everett regain his balance.

"What do you mean the ring worked? This ring?" he asked, as he looked down at the ring Everett had forced upon him.

"Yes, that ring. Come on, we'll talk as we walk. We can't stay here."

Michael took one last look at the old magician's enclave, now Acantha's keep, before turning to chase after Everett.

"What kind of magic was that, Everett?" he called, as he hurried after the old magician.

"That," Everett said when Michael caught up to him, "was the power that you are capable of --- doubled."

"Doubled?"

"Yes. The emerald ring is a talisman that enhances the wearer's abilities. There are two rings. You have one, the other is a ruby ring. Acantha has that one."

Michael stopped and shook his head in confusion. "Why? Why would Acantha do this? She had everyone in the enclave killed. She's my sister, why would she do such a thing?"

Michael caught up with Everett and tugged on his shoulder, turning him around. "Everett, what in the hell is going on here? You know what's happening. You have to tell me. I'm stuck right in the middle and I don't understand what's going on."

Everett put up his hands to ward off Michael's barrage of questions. "Okay, okay. But keep walking. We'll talk as we travel."

Michael sighed in frustration. "For an old man that was worn out just a few minutes ago, you sure got your energy back fast enough."

"It is imperative we get away from here. Let's go."

They continued walking down the hill. In less than three miles, they approached the shores of the great western ocean and headed north. The terrain here below the San Simeon hills was flat and gentle. It was still early in the day, and before nightfall they would begin to reach the area of the coastline that was as rugged and treacherous as it was beautiful.

"Where are we going?" asked Michael.

"To the Cruz Mountains. You'll love it there, lush greenery high over the coast. You can see for miles."

"Well, considering the situation I can't be overly excited about the scenery. I mean, we just barely survive the worst carnage either of us has ever seen, everyone at the enclave is murdered, my sister, Acantha, is possessed by some powerful evil force that I don't begin to understand."

Everett frowned at Michael. "I know that, Michael. We are not going north on holiday. We are fleeing for our lives, albeit slowly. We should be safe by the time we reach the village of Monterey. We are going to the Cruz Mountains not to relish in the beauty of the land, but rather, so that you can meditate and strengthen your puny powers. Then, perhaps, you will be able to master the magic that can be channeled to you through that emerald ring."

"Sorry, Everett. It's just that I'm confused, and I must confess more than a little frightened."

Everett softened a bit. "I know, Michael. But, it's time for you to accept responsibilities that you have shirked in the past. You have neglected your studies of the magical arts, barely passing your apprentice exams. You preferred to chase the daughters of the head groundskeeper. Your lack of diligence and serious study was irritating before, but if you don't grow up immediately it will be much worse that irritating, it will be deadly."

He smiled and patted Michael on the shoulder as they continued to walk north. "I'm sorry if I seem to be coming down a bit hard on you, but it really is a matter of life and death. You must leave the frivolity of youth behind you for a while."

After a couple of miles of steady walking, they finally allowed themselves a few minutes rest. The two men made their way down to the beach where Everett unceremoniously plopped down to the warm sand and stretched out. It was hours into the afternoon now, but since it was late summer they still had sunlight left.

"My god but I'm exhausted!"

"I thought you were doing pretty good, Everett. You seemed to have plenty of energy."

"A little spell helped to sustain my energy level. Unfortunately I pay for it with exhaustion when it wears off."

"I didn't see you place a spell," remarked Michael.

"You weren't paying attention. And you haven't studied hard enough to have noticed it.

"No, No," he continued quickly. "I'm not scolding, merely making an observation," the teacher said.

Everett sat up and removed his soft leather boots so that he could rub his tired and aching feet.

"Ah, that's better."

"So, you said you were going to tell me about these rings. Where did they come from, why are they so powerful, and how did Acantha come to have them?"

"Well," began Everett. "I'm not sure how closely you listened in your classes about the history of magic, so I'll probably tell you some things that you already know.

"Before there was magic in this world, there was what was called energy and technology. While we still have the natural sciences, we have lost the mechanical sciences. That would be energy and technology. The sciences where man was capable of producing..."

"Yeah, I know," interrupted Michael. "People were able to do all kinds of things without magic. They had machines large and small that traveled over the land on their own power. Even machines that carried people in their bellies and flew through the air like birds."

"Ah, so, you did listen to at least some of your history. Then magic came into the world. No one knows how it happened, but the world lost its technology and energy, and gained magic."

"And then the Magicians' War, right?" asked Michael.

"Yes, the Magicians' War. After magic came into the world the leaders found that their engines of war no longer worked. Well, rather than resigning themselves to the unacceptable concept of peace, they formed armies of the most powerful magicians."

"And nearly destroyed the world, right?"

"With the aid of the talismans of magic, yes. There are certain items that channel magic and focus their powers to maximum strength."

Everett pointed at the ring on Michael's finger. "That ring and the ruby ring that Acantha now wears are two of the strongest talismans. At the end of the Magicians' War both rings were worn by the same person and used as a weapon of war. It ended the war and nearly destroyed mankind. There used to be millions of people just in this country alone. By comparison, only a handful are left. I told you that the emerald ring doubled your power. If you wore both of them at the same time, your powers would be strengthened ten-fold."

Michael looked at the ring on his finger with newly found respect. "So, that's why it was so important that Acantha not have both rings. Her power would be strengthened ten-fold." He looked up at the old magician with hurt in his eyes. "But, I don't understand why Acantha did what she did. She wasn't evil before this, and no one could do what she did without being evil. What happened to her?"

"What happened to her has to do with why you have never heard of these talismans before. The magician's enclave was founded in part to teach the art of magic to aspiring students, but another function of the enclave was to safeguard the talismans. Only the teachers knew of their existence. They are entirely too powerful to allow them to fall into the wrong hands. What makes them so dangerous is that the ruby ring channels evil power."

"Then Acantha wasn't evil until she slipped that ring on."

"That's right. If she had slipped the emerald ring on first, none of this would have happened."

"Well, if only the teachers knew about the rings, how did Acantha wind up with them?"

Everett thought for a moment before replying. "Perhaps a more important question is how are we going to get the ruby away from her now? I was lucky to get the emerald. I surprised her, I don't expect to be able to do that again."

"Maybe we should just leave things as they are. I mean – she doesn't have both of them now, and if we get far enough away..."

"No, I know what you're thinking, Michael. But she will not rest until she has both rings."

Michael looked back in the quickening darkness toward the old enclave. It was out of sight now, but he could pinpoint where it would be, just over one of the largest hills. Instead of the warmth and security one should feel when looking toward home, all he could feel was fear and coldness.

\* \* \* \* \*

Acantha stood glaring into the warm afternoon sun. She was standing on the balcony of the highest tower of the old magician's enclave. She was leaning over the balcony railing, watching as best she could Croom's attack and Michael's surprising defense. She was gripping the railing so hard that her knuckles were turning even whiter than the alabaster skin of her hands.

"Incompetent lout!" she yelled. She was much too far for Croom to hear her, even if he were alive, which he obviously was not. Still, she could not help but vent her rage at the man that had let her down and thwarted her goals.

"Look at them! They're getting away!" she shouted. She was shouting at no one, as there was no one left alive at the enclave. She had to watch helplessly as her quarry escaped down the hill. There was no one left to send after them, and she was not willing to sully her own hands, at least not yet.

"I'm not ready to let you off the hook yet, you fool." She pounded the stone railing as she focused on Croom once more. "I'll bring you back. Yes, that's what I'll do! I know I can. With the power I now possess, and the knowledge that is held in the library, I know that I can bring you back to life."

She turned from the scene on the hillside and rushed back into her new keep. She was giddy with her new powers and her freshly-hatched plan to bring Croom back to life through necromancy. She giggled and complemented herself on her intelligence and insight as she ran down staircase after staircase until she reached the ground floor. With silken dress flowing behind her, she dashed out the door and down the hill to where lay Croom's crumpled corpse.

She was still laughing gaily when she arrived at the spot on the hill where the short but furious battle had taken place. A scowl replaced her smiling face when she saw closely what had become of her deadly servant.

"You see what has happened to you. And just because you are a fool." She pointed an accusing finger at Croom's torn and battered body.

"Well, don't worry. You failed because you were a fool. I'll make you so that you cannot be defeated. You will not be able to be killed because, of course, you are already quite dead."

Once again she began her quiet little selfish laugh. "Come along now and I will see what I can do about fixing you up some. You really are quite a mess."

With a negligent wave of her hand, Croom's body began to quiver and stir. Acantha turned from the dead man and began walking back up the hill to her keep. The corpse followed five feet behind, rolling and tumbling through the dust and brush with every step she made.

Acantha was quite unconcerned about whether her spell had worked; nor was she concerned about the gouges or torn flesh the corpse was receiving from its rough treatment. She was confident that the awesome power given to her by the ruby would ensure any spell that she performed and that it would be strong enough to repair Croom's battered body when she brought it back to life.

"Who's going to do all my work now that you're a stupid corpse?" she muttered as she continued to trudge up the hill. The good humor that she was feeling about her new plan was leaving her now that she had to exert some real energy herself.

"I'm going to need some help around here. I'm going to be much too busy regaining the emerald and then asserting my will on an inferior people. I won't have time to do the boring chores like cooking and cleaning."

She turned around and pointed another accusing finger at the torn and battered body rolling through the dirt after her. "If you had done what I told you to do, I wouldn't have to worry about all of these mundane things."

She continued her walk back to the keep as she continued talking to herself. "Supply boat. That's it. There is a supply boat due in a few days. The supply boats have all kinds of seamen that I can recruit to be my servants."

With her mind clear on how she would handle the day-to-day chore of running the large castle, she returned her attention to the plan of bringing Croom back to life.

She left him lying of the floor of the main hall as she retired to the massive library to begin her search for the right spells.

"Yes, Croom, I think Michael and Everett will be very surprised to see you again."

CHAPTER 2

It took Michael and Everett weeks of travel to reach the small village of Monterey. The village was situated across the bay from Cruztown and the Cruz Mountains. It was decided that Everett would travel on to the Cruz Mountains while Michael stayed in Monterey for a short time. Since Michael was the younger and stronger, he would work at whatever manual labor he could find to earn enough credits to buy supplies for the two of them.

"Are you sure we should be out here in this kind of weather, Karl?" Michael was asking the question of the man sitting across from him in the small fishing boat.

Late summer storms were a rarity, but when they struck they could be very fierce. This particular storm caught Michael and the owner of the small boat early in the morning as they were first setting out to fish the bay. The other fishermen were smart enough that they did not even consider setting out in this weather, but Karl's greed was too strong.

The small boat was rocking wildly in the rough surf less than a half mile from the rocky shore. The two men each had an oar and were laboring to keep the boat prow-first into the waves.

"Look, who's the boss on this boat?" By now the wind was blowing so hard and the rain coming in sheets that Karl was nearly shouting, even though they were sitting right next to each other.

"Well, you are, but..."

"Yeah, and who's going to pay you the credits for working on this boat?"

"Well, you are, but..."

"And which one of us here is the experienced fisherman of this bay?"

"I guess you are, but..."

"Then shut up and row!"

In fact, Karl had been fishing the bay less than a year. No one knew from where he had drifted into town. If any of the townsfolk had known more about him, they would have known that he had very little experience with the sea or working a boat. What little success he had with his fishing came from listening to the other fishermen and doing what they did, and following them to wherever the fish were to be found.

Which made some sense in normal conditions, but not when it came to dangerous weather. It was Karl's arrogance that had led him into this situation. No amount of experience would have justified being on the water in a storm such as this.

"I don't know, Karl," hollered Michael over the wind and rain. "I think it's getting worse! I think maybe we should go back!"

Karl was too busy manning his own oar to respond to Michael. He was finally beginning to realize that he was woefully lacking in the skill necessary to handle this situation.

"Okay!" He yelled back at Michael. "If you can't handle it, we'll go back!" Inwardly he thanked his lucky stars that he could turn back and blame it on Michael, while showing himself in the favorable light of caring about his worker's safety.

In an attempt to return to shore, Karl's lack of experience caused him to turn the boat broadside into a wave. As he turned the boat, one of the wild waves came crashing over the low sides – hitting Michael with enough force to rip him from his bench and toss him overboard, cracking his head on the flying oar. Karl was protected from the main force of the wave because it hit Michael and he was able to hold onto his side of the boat without being thrown overboard.

Karl did not give a second thought to Michael as the young man went flying past him and into the roiling ocean. He was too busy holding on for dear life and blaming Michael for getting him into this mess by making him turn back. The next wave took Karl over the side and down to the bottom of the raging sea, where he paid the ultimate price for his arrogance.

Without knowing how he got there, Michael found himself engulfed in the cold and violent ocean. He felt as though each time he fought his way above the surface of the water to gasp a breath of air, a giant angry hand would swat him back under a wave. With quickly flagging strength, Michael would have to fight his way back up all over again. The blow to the head, and the confusion and disorientation made it impossible to use his magic.

He was barely conscious and nearly overcome with exhaustion when he finally heard the waves crashing on the rocky shore. Using all of his remaining energy, Michael struggled toward the sound of the booming surf.

He barely sensed that his ravaged body was being thrown violently among the rocks on the shore until he felt himself slammed into the hard black stones. He finally passed out from pain and fatigue.

*    *    *    *    *

That night, with the storm still blowing, Sarah finally convinced the last of her patrons that it was time to leave her tavern and go home for the night.

Sarah was the owner and operator of the fishermen's favorite tavern in Monterey. She was a bit shorter than medium height, a slim girl with shoulder length blonde hair framing a delicate face. Her light blue eyes were almost too large for her pixie appearance.

Since the storm had brought them in early, most of the fishermen had met at Sarah's to tell tall tales of the sea, and to see who could boast the loudest and tell the most outrageous lie.

Sarah's was a large old tavern, cluttered with obscure useless relics from a time no one remembered. The barroom was dark from too few windows, and the tables were old and worn with not even the benefit of a cloth to cover them. Even so, it was a spotlessly clean and comfortable place.

Sarah was approaching the door to lock up for the night when Michael half staggered and half fell through the tavern doorway. His stumbling steps sent him reeling into her and the collision took them both to the floor. His long black hair was matted with blood and plastered against his scalp, his face was pallid, his eyes hollow.

She did not realize what had happened until Charlie, her simple-minded helper, separated the injured man and Sarah from the tangled heap.

"Are you all right, Miss Sarah?"

Sarah was dazed, sitting on the floor just inside the door, with the wind and rain blowing in on her. Her arms were propped up behind her and her legs were splayed out with her skirt immodestly thrown above her knees.

"What in the world...?"

Charlie gently laid the stranger aside and rushed to close the door before Sarah became soaked to the bone.

"This fellow here is a mess! He came crashing through the door and fell right on top of you. You both went down. Splat!"

Sarah looked over at the unmoving pile of soaking wet rags that Charlie said was a man. A stranger in as much of a mess as this fellow seemed to be usually meant trouble, but Sarah was too kind-hearted to throw the injured man back out into the storm. She had Charlie carry him to the back room where she lived, while she bolted the door and window shutters.

When she returned to her room, she found that Charlie had already made the stranger comfortable on the bed and was washing the blood and grime from his face.

She saw that the unconscious young man was quite handsome. He was about her age, late teens or early twenties, with straight black hair, tanned complexion, and a tall, muscular body. Perhaps his nose was too sharply defined and the mouth too generous, but put all together it worked quite well.

"Who is he, Charlie? Have you ever seen him before?"

"No, ma'am. Must be new 'round here. I know nearly everyone in town, and he ain't one of 'em."

"Yeah," said Sarah, with a little smile, "and those that you don't know, I do."

Sarah looked closely at the man's head now that Charlie had it clean. He had taken a grievous cut above the left temple.

"You had better get me a clean sheet that I can make some bandages from," she said to Charlie as she examined Michael's wound. "Then you can go get Oliver for me."

Oliver was an old fisherman and Sarah's self-appointed protector. He had been watching after the young woman ever since her uncle had died.

She thought of her Uncle Gus often. He had always been the center of her world, the only family she had. She remembered a strong, happy man that loved and cared for her. He had played games with her when she was a little girl, and taught her everything that he could to help prepare her for adulthood.

When she was older and helping him with the tavern by making sandwiches and serving the patrons, he was her protector. More than a few migrant seamen found themselves face down in the dusty street outside the bar when they tried to become too friendly with Sarah.

The word was eventually spread not to tamper with old Gus's niece. Now that Gus was no longer around, Oliver and the other fishermen and dock workers that frequented the tavern cared for and protected Sarah. Occasional migrant seamen still found themselves rolling in the dust in front of the tavern.

Over the next few days, Sarah and her friends were able to nurse Michael back to good health. As his healing continued, Sarah found more reasons than necessary to go to his bedside and see that he was properly cared for.

For Michael's part, he told Sarah that he and his old friend were traveling north, but did not mention anything about the magician's enclave or that he was a magician himself. Because of the Magicians' War, and the cataclysmic results, magicians were feared and avoided.

As Michael recovered from his ordeal, Sarah spent all the time she could being near him. Walking together along the quiet lapping surf one evening, Michael was struck with how gentle the ocean was compared to the morning that he had nearly drowned.

"The ocean was so wild that morning," he told Sarah, as he stared out at the moon's reflection on the water.

"It's smooth tonight," she answered with a smile.

Michael returned her smile. "I think you have a calming effect on it."

"Oh, right. I tamed the ocean, is that it?"

"I think you could." Michael pulled her close to him, gently pressing his lips to hers.

Sarah's heart was beating so strongly that she was sure Michael could hear it over the surf. When their lips finally parted she needed a few seconds to catch her breath before she could speak.

"Don't play with me, Michael."

"I'm not playing," he answered, as he pulled her into a tight embrace.

"Will you stay here with me instead of going north?"

"I want to. I want to very much."

"Then stay."

Michael could not tell her about the reasons that were causing him to travel north. The only answer that he could give her was to hold her closer. He understood his responsibilities in keeping the emerald ring from Acantha, but he had been here a few weeks and had heard nothing from her or seen any signs that she was pursuing him and Everett.

He made his decision. He would stay here with Sarah. If Acantha would leave him alone, he would leave her alone. Everything that he ever wanted was standing right there in his arms.

"So?" asked Sarah.

"What?"

She sighed and pushed him away.

"So will you stay? Will you stay here with me, or are you going to continue traveling?"

Michael smiled down at her.

"If it's at all possible, I'll stay. I don't ever want to leave you now that I have found you."

She sighed once again, this time in pleasure and melted back into his arms.

"We can have a nice peaceful life here," she said.

CHAPTER 3

Sarah glanced nervously at the table in the corner. It was occupied by a short thick man with a heavy jaw and brow. His mouth was thin and straight with the corners slanting down, as if by nature it had never been meant to smile. He tried to push his dirty thinning hair down with stubby fingers as he watched the few patrons. Sounds of raucous laughter would flow over to the strange man's table, the table which, Sarah noticed, all the rough seafaring men avoided looking at, without knowing why.

Sarah hoped that Charlie would be here before long to work the evening hours. If he got here soon enough she would not have to go near the stranger again. He was causing no trouble that she could see, she just felt uncomfortable around the dirty man.

She was supposed to meet Michael at the old building on the hill where he spent most of his time. The going was quite rough and she did not want to make the walk without strong light.

Within minutes Charlie ambled in the front door.

"Hi, Sarah," Charlie called out. He was wearing his normal foolish grin as he approached. "A lotta work for me tonight," he said, as he reached the bar. "Ships from the south due in tomorrow, and I gotta be ready for a full bar tomorrow night."

"Oh, Charlie, I forgot about that. Do you want me to stay behind tonight to help you get ready?"

"No, ma'am! Don't need no help."

"I just thought it would make it easier for you if I stayed."

"No, ma'am! I'll have this place up to snuff before I leave here tonight, don't you worry none."

"I never worry when you're here, Charlie. All right, I guess I'll quit for the night." She glanced again at the strange man at the corner table.

Charlie gave Sarah another grin. "Yes, ma'am, you go ahead now. I'm sure you want to meet up with Michael."

Charlie didn't have to convince Sarah that he would be able to manage the tavern without her. She knew that. She gave the stranger one final look as she left for the evening.

Her mood was light and a smile was on her face as she made her walk through the village. Even the shambles of Monterey seemed beautiful to her. No doubt it was a beautiful city in times past, but now showed the haphazard architecture of neglect. Most of the city was composed of shards of ancient fallen buildings, overgrown with a jungle of trees and bushes.

The city had obviously been home to thousands of people once, but now, after the Magicians' War, only a few hundred people lived in Monterey. They claimed whatever surviving buildings they could as their own. Most of the people lived in the center of the city not far from the ocean. Here they could be together near the docks where the small ruggedly-built wooden ships would arrive with supplies brought from the south. The supplies would be bartered for food that was grown in the lush valley, a day's journey inland.

Sarah reached the building where Michael spent most of his time. It was located just a short walk from the docks of Monterey. There were other buildings nearby, but not nearly as many as in the center of the village. The hulks that remained stood empty and added an aspect of loneliness to the hillside where they lived. The area was overgrown with trees and shrubbery.

In the failing light, Sarah followed the path through the woods that led to the door of the low building. The entire front wall had at one time contained large panels of glass. Most of the windows were boarded up where the glass was missing. Only three of the windows still retained the ancient glass.

She entered the building. The first room inside was cavernous. Throughout the room was a large number of old wooden desks and chairs and along the walls were crumbling shelves filled with old books. Not just a few, but hundreds, maybe thousands of books. Most were unreadable and would crumble when touched, but some were still in good enough condition. This was Michael's favorite room.

Sarah's reading abilities were poor at best, although her uncle had taught her enough to operate the business. She quickly found that was not enough to wade through the massive volumes that Michael always kept in front of him. She quickly tired of the books and even their pictures. They were of people, places, and things she could not comprehend. Michael would spend hours in this room reading about ancient times and ancient places. It all seemed quite useless to Sarah.

Farther back in the building were other rooms also filled with shelves of the books, and more of the old wooden desks.

Upon entering, she saw Michael sitting at one of the desks with a large book open in front of him. The room was lit by one large candle on his table. Next to him was the crossbow and bolts that Oliver had insisted he keep with him when he made these trips into the woods. As evening fell, the wilder animals would become bolder and Sarah's friends wanted to be sure that he could protect her if the need arose.

She felt warm and loved as she quietly crossed the room to Michael's side. He jumped as he became aware of her next to him. She laughed lightly at him as she bent down to kiss him on the cheek.

"What are you reading about now?" she asked.

"Another country," he answered as he returned her kiss. "It's on the other side of the world."

"Sounds very interesting." She gave a mock yawn and patted her mouth to show her boredom.

"I can tell you're overcome with excitement."

"So how long before you're ready to go?"

"Oh, I guess we could..."

Sarah screamed as the wooden door behind her burst from its rusty hinges. Outlined against the darkening sky, lit only by the dull glow of the single candle, she could see the silhouette of a short thick man. As he stalked across the room she recognized him as the stranger from the bar. The man everyone avoided. The man that had made her feel so uncomfortable. He was thickly muscled, wearing dirty traveling clothes, his head and face stained with the grime that revealed a hard journey. He must have spent a month, maybe more, of traveling the roads and forests, sleeping in the open. She wondered if this man bothered with sleep. All these thoughts flashed through her mind in a moment, the time it took the assassin to reach the center of the room.

"You know you can't deny me," rasped the apparition. "Acantha would see you dead. I am here to do her bidding."

As the intruder took another lumbering step toward the pair, Michael grabbed the crossbow beside him, and with a strength aided by terror, wrenched the bowstring back and fitted a bolt in place with a speed that would have astonished him, had he a moment to consider it. In vain desperation, Michael barely paused to aim as he fired the weapon at his attacker. The bolt sprang from the bow as Sarah shrank from the violence. The assassin crashed to the floor as the bolt buried into his chest nearly to the fletching. Sarah gaped at the fallen assassin with terror in her eyes.

Her terror intensified as the would-be slayer lurched to his feet, the bolt protruding from his chest in mocking defiance of the one who shot it. Not a drop of blood could be seen on his grimy tunic. As he continued his ponderous advance toward them, Michael grabbed Sarah by the arm, pulling her with him as he fled the room. If he moved quickly enough, and they could escape from the building before the assassin reached them, he thought, perhaps they might have a chance.

Sarah raced through the rear of the building in confusion and blind terror, her arm still tightly clasped in Michael's iron grip. A part of her mind could still hear the assassin blundering through the dark building behind them.

Shelves of ancient books, chairs and desks were being dodged or toppled in their haste. Behind her she could hear the crashing destruction as the stranger tried to shove his way through the unfamiliar building. Rather than passing smoothly around obstacles, as

Michael and Sarah did, the maniac seemed to prefer to smash through everything in his way.

Sara charged into Michael before she could see he had stopped. They were outdoors now, having escaped through the rear door. Barely ten yards beyond the building, they were canopied by the unconcerned forest and the twinkling of the first stars of the night.

Michael dropped his crossbow on the ground beside him and let loose of Sarah's arm, his hands moving to the sides of his head, eyes wide and staring. He spun and faced the building. Sarah could see the assassin approaching the doorway. She recoiled as the building filled with a vibrant green light and imploded with a force that knocked her off her feet.

She barely had time to catch her breath before Michael pulled her to her feet and they were running toward the forest. Still in the midst of confusion, she did not hear his question until he repeated it.

"We need help and supplies, will Oliver help us? Sarah?"

"What? Oh...Oliver; yes, of course, Oliver will help us."

They stopped running and slowed to a walk when Sarah began gasping for breath. Her fear finally overcame the confusion when she thought of the sinister man that had attacked them and his unstoppable onslaught.

It was dark now and a heavy wet fog began to enclose them, heightening the dread of the night. The silence and the closeness of the overgrown woods and thick brush gave life to Sarah's panicked imagination. Soon she felt death and destruction was concealed around every turn of the path, hidden behind every shadowy tree.

Inside the fallen building, the assassin was clawing at the rubble that held him from his quarry.

## CHAPTER 4

As shock replaced confusion and terror, Sarah began shaking as though chilled. Michael wrapped his woolen cloak about her shoulders and they continued toward town. They walked through the unnaturally peaceful forest for just a few minutes before Sarah spoke.

"What in the world happened back there, Michael? What's going on?"

Michael ran his fingers through his fog-dampened hair and sighed. He looked behind him and shook his head as he continued to lead Sarah out of the forest and back into town.

"It's such a long and confusing story. I don't know how or where to begin."

"Well, how about at the beginning. Who was that madman, and why did he want to kill you?"

She slowed almost to a stop as she asked her questions.

"Come on," urged Michael gently. "Keep walking. I'll tell you all I can when we get to Oliver's. I don't want to be around here when he gets out of that building."

"When he gets out of the building?!" she exclaimed. "What are you talking about? Surely he's dead. That whole building collapsed on top of him. He's buried underneath all that rubble with your crossbow bolt in his chest. You don't really believe he's going to survive that, do you?"

"Well, survive is not quite the right word. Look, just believe me that it's important that we get away from here. I'll explain everything at Oliver's."

Sarah pulled her gaze from Michael's pleading face and peered at the eerily quiet forest surrounding them.

"I give up. We'll go on to Oliver's, but then I want to know what's happening."

It was nearly ten minutes later when the two frightened young people approached the end of the wildly overgrown forest.

During the short trip to the village, Michael was berating himself for putting Sarah in such danger. He had no right to drag her into this. And now Croom, or Acantha through Croom, knew about Sarah and would use her to get to him. Everett had told him that Acantha would stop at nothing to regain the emerald, and Michael had just seen the proof of that.

How was he going to explain all of this to Sarah? Further, how was he going to explain it to Oliver? Oliver had always been Sarah's chief protector. He wasn't going to be pleased with Michael. If he could persuade Oliver to help them reach the Cruz Mountains, his old teacher would help them.

There was another problem. He had not told Sarah that he was a magician. Magicians were not held in high regard. The only thing that people knew about magicians was that they nearly destroyed the world in another age.

Would Sarah understand or would she draw away from him when he told her that he was an apprentice magician? He didn't like the fact that he had hidden this from her, but it hardly made sense to go around bragging about something that everyone else viewed with fear and superstition.

As they finally walked out from the forest into the village, Sarah was struck by the sinister aspect of the town that she had known so well. The terror of the night made her aware of how strange the tall buildings were. Some were still standing complete, but most were just hulks of what they must have been. Row after row of darkened, glassless windows glared defiantly. So many buildings, so many rooms. What kind of people could have built such structures? How could they have managed such a thing?

Everywhere there were rusted and crumbling metal wagons that the people of those days used for travel. Heavy cumbersome relics. These old hulks, Michael had told her, had at one time traveled under their own power without the need for horses to pull them. How could that be? They just squatted where they were as if they had been there from the beginning of time; sitting there as if they were a decrepit joke left by their ancestors.

All of these things she had seen before, but had never paid any real attention to. Now everywhere Sarah looked were reminders of a time that was dead. Reminders of a world that was dead. She shuddered to think such thoughts on this night of all nights.

They continued toward the docks, across the cracked and broken ancient concrete that had been made for those strange metal wagons. As they approached Oliver's old cabin, they were both aware of the stillness in the air. It was as if the entire waterfront was aware of the deadly assassin that had invaded their peaceful village, and everyone had all locked themselves behind closed doors and shuttered windows to disavow any responsibility for the dangers that threatened.

In truth, the graveyard quiet was the result of hard working men and women that retired with the sun. This part of the town was inhabited by the fishermen that would be up before dawn to put in a hard day's work before the rest of the town was stirring.

Within a stone's throw from the edge of the shoreline they had constructed several rough wooden structures for living space, using salvaged wood and unknown harder substances from the deserted buildings in the village. The appearance was of temporary shacks, thrown up hurriedly.

These were rugged men who cared not for beauty in their homes, but in strength and durability to withstand the few, but harsh, winter storms that would batter the coast.

Oliver's cabin was just such a structure; strong and durable despite the old weather-beaten appearance. He would have been surprised to hear that a description of his cabin could have been used to describe him as well.

Not a handsome man, he had deep creases born from the harsh ocean winds covering his worn face and a nose that looked as though it would be more at home in a potato field rather than in the middle of someone's face. His body, though more ample than might be necessary, was strong. The hardness of his muscles was the result of a lifetime on the waters, plying his trade. In spite of Oliver's rough exterior, his kindness and gentle spirit showed in his soft brown eyes. The softness of his eyes was balanced by strong jutting brows that suggested one should be careful of pushing this gentle man too far.

He had been sleeping soundly when the persistent knocking roused him. He did not feel alarmed as he stumbled through the darkened interior, but rather confused that someone would be at his door at such a late hour.

It would be useless for thieves to come to the door of a fisherman's shack as there was nothing to steal, and even less likely that they would knock. Oliver had no enemies, so it was with a sleepy smile that he opened the door to his friends. His smile was replaced with a concerned look when he saw Sarah, obviously frightened and confused.

"Good heavens child, come on in. Just stand there while I light a lamp."

Michael stood with a protective arm around Sarah, just inside the entrance to the old shack, while Oliver lit the oil lamps. It was a typical fisherman's shack littered with cork, pieces of netting, various tools for keeping his boat in operating condition, and other tools of his trade. The walls were covered with shelving containing random shells, polished driftwood, carvings, and an abundance of dust. Where the floors met with the walls there was similar clutter. Worthless keepsakes of a man that had lived alone, seemingly forever.

Once the lamps were lit Michael led Sarah to an old wooden table with benches on either side, where they sat to wait for the inevitable questions that needed to be answered.

"So, what is this, child?" asked Oliver, as he joined them at the table. "You look badly frightened. What happened?" He brought three mugs of tea, still warm from the old wood burning stove in the corner that was providing heat in the cabin.

Michael quickly explained to Oliver what had happened. When he had completed the telling of the attack, he told them both of the urgency to leave Monterey.

"I don't quite understand the need to run any further, Michael. It sounds as though the fellow that attacked you is quite dead. Of course, I'd like to know what caused the building to collapse at such an opportune time."

Michael stopped to gather his thoughts as he rubbed his face with both hands. "This fellow, as you call him, that attacked us is dead all right. But he was already dead when he burst through the front door. I killed him myself a couple of months ago!"

Sarah threw her arms up in despair. "I give up, Michael. Life was very normal for me up until about an hour ago. What do you mean he was already dead? How in the world could a dead man be walking, talking, and trying to kill you? He said Acantha had sent him. Who is Acantha? Why does she want you dead?"

"Well, I'm trying to explain," continued Michael. "I just need to think about how to say it all."

Oliver gave Michael a stern look as he leaned across the table. "Form your thoughts if you have to, but I think it's about time you got to the truth. Start at the beginning."

Michael took a deep breath to steel his nerves before plunging ahead with the story that could cause both of his friends to turn against him.

"The man who attacked us, if you wish to call him a man, is controlled through sorcery. Croom was his name. When I knew him, he was at his best when he was bullying or tyrannizing someone. Now...well, what better role for him to play than a ghoul."

"Sorcery! But why you, Michael," interrupted Sarah. "Why is he trying to kill you? And who is this Acantha that sent him after you?"

Michael sighed. "Do you know anything about the magician's enclave that was south of here?"

Sarah said she did not, but Oliver, having traveled up and down the entire coast, did.

"Yeah, I've heard of it. There's a whole nest of those magicians down there doing heaven only knows what," he spat.

"Well, there's no nest of magicians now," Michael continued tentatively, "that's where I came from before I showed up here in Monterey. It was there that I killed Croom. He's the man that just attacked us," he added.

"Wait a minute!" cried Sarah as she lurched to her feet. "Are you saying that you're a magician?"

"Well...yes. I was a learning member at the enclave. I was an apprentice of magic, as was my sister. My sister is Acantha."

"Heavens, Michael!" continued Sarah. "You killed a man a few months ago who isn't really dead, and now he's trying to kill you, and you're telling me you're a magician and your sister is a sorceress!"

Oliver slumped in his chair as if greatly disappointed. "Not just any sorceress, mind you," he said quietly, "but Acantha. I've heard tales of her recently from the seamen who come into port. She's been capturing the crews from ships that come too close to shore. Now no one in their right mind goes near that castle she lives in."

Oliver suddenly sat erect and slammed his fist down on the table with a force that knocked Michael's cup of tea into the air. When it landed, it was on its side with the contents spilling across the table. Michael nearly jumped out of his seat.

"I had hopes for you, boy," Oliver grated. "I've watched over Sarah as if she were my own ever since her Uncle Gus died. Now you have put her in a danger that could have been avoided. If I had known what I know now, I would have chased you out of town the first time I laid eyes on you." Anger built up in him. "A frigging' magician! How could you have fallen for a magician, Sarah?"

"I didn't know he was a magician," answered Sarah, confused and upset. When she saw the fallen look on Michael's face she instinctively wanted to protect him in spite of what she had just learned. "I'm sorry, Michael. I didn't mean it like that, but why didn't you tell me before?"

"Because of the fear and superstition everyone feels about magic. Because of the fear you're showing right now."

"With good cause, seems to me," said Oliver, as he glared at Michael.

"This is getting us nowhere," said Sarah quickly as she regained her seat next to Michael. "Let's leave all of the blaming until we hear the rest of the story."

Oliver left the table to get a cloth to clean the spilled tea. When he returned he tossed the cloth to Michael. "O.K., go ahead. We're listening."

Michael blotted the tea from the table as he continued his tale. "Acantha wasn't always feared. She used to be a good person. Someone you would like to have for a sister."

"Right," snorted Oliver sarcastically.

Michael took another deep breath before resuming. He had known this was not going to be easy, but now that he was facing Oliver, he wished he were anywhere other than in front of Sarah's chief protector.

"Let me go back a bit so you can understand what happened, and what is happening now."

Michael told Sarah and Oliver how the magicians at the enclave were charged with the hiding and protection of the talismans of magic, and how Acantha had stolen the rings and been possessed by the evil powers of the ruby ring.

"There were two rings," he continued. "One was the ruby ring I told you about and the other was an emerald ring. This emerald ring."

Michael raised his right hand to show them the beautiful emerald ring he was wearing.

"I've never noticed that before," said Sarah quietly, as she leaned over to get a closer look at the large ring.

"One of its special qualities, it seems," responded Michael. "I've worn it every day that we've been together, and you never noticed it."

"So," interrupted Oliver, "this Croom guy is trying to kill you to get that ring back for your sister?"

"That's about it," responded Michael.

"Yeah, right," Oliver continued sarcastically, "she sounds just like the sister I've always wanted."

Michael sighed, "I told you, it's not her doing all this, it's the ruby that has taken her over. It's just like the two times the emerald took me over and saved my life through its magic."

Oliver stood and stretched with arms wide. "Okay, at least you managed to get Sarah here where she will be safe. I'll help you get out of town so you can clean up this mess away from here."

"I'm afraid that won't be enough now," Michael tentatively offered. "If I leave Sarah here, now that Acantha knows about her, Acantha will take her and use her to get to me. It's true I have to leave, but Sarah must come with me."

"No!" snapped Oliver, and he dismissed Michael's suggestion with a wave of the hand. "I won't allow it. She's never been out of the village before, and now you want to pick her up and run off with her, while some monster of a man is following you. Not a chance. My friends and I will see to her safety. I'm not letting her run off with some magician!"

It was Sarah who first recovered from Oliver's tirade. "Oliver, you are the oldest and dearest friend I have, but I love Michael. Where he goes, I go! We had hoped for your help, not your judgment."

Sarah got up from the table and pulled on Michael's arm as though it was time to go.

When Michael stood, Oliver quickly recanted. "Wait a minute. Wait a minute."

He thought quickly while they stood waiting expectantly.

"Okay, you win. Sit down so we can figure what to do next."

The young couple returned to the table. Everyone was now more subdued than when the Sarah and Michael had burst in on the sleeping Oliver. Oliver pushed his now-cold mug of tea away and moved his chair back from the table. He paused to rub his jaw with a gnarled hand as he looked at Michael.

"So, what do you plan to do? Do you have a safe place where you can go?"

Michael told Oliver about his old friend and teacher, Everett, and how Everett was waiting for him across the bay in the Cruz Mountains.

"Then your first problem is getting from here to there without this Croom fellow following right on your heels," said Oliver. "I don't understand how this sister of yours could manage to raise a dead man from his grave, magic or no magic, but I'll do all I can to help. Not for you, mind you! But for Sarah.

"We will dress you two up in some old fishing clothes I have around here and set out with the fleet in the morning. When we get out from shore, we'll separate from the rest of the fleet and head over to Cruz Town. We'll be in the mountains before your assassin even knows how you got out of town.

"Now, we get you to the Cruz Mountains; what then? Do you know where to find this old magician?"

"I've never been to the Cruz Mountains," Michael replied. "And I don't know where to start looking for him. But remember, he is a very strong magician. Even if I'm a rather poor excuse for an apprentice, we'll find him once we get to the mountains, or he'll find us."

"Well, I'm coming with you two kids," said Oliver. He turned to look at Sarah. "I'm not going to leave your welfare to a magician, no matter how much you love him. Besides, I promised your uncle on his death bed I would watch out for you and that is exactly what I am going to do!"

"Oliver, no," objected Sarah. "I can't let you put yourself in danger like that. You just heard what we are up against. If you can just get us across the bay. We can go on alone from there."

"Don't you start worrying about me, girl," he replied as he began gathering clothing and supplies. "You may consider me over the hill, but a man that has worked this ocean for thirty years the way I have builds up strength to put you land-locked folk to shame."

"While you two are arguing," interrupted Michael, "I'm going to slip outside for a short time. If we're not leaving for a few hours yet, we need a shield around us so Croom won't know we're here. I think it's time for my magic to come out of retirement."

CHAPTER 5

Croom's persistent effort against the rubble was finally rewarded. The darkness of the fallen building was replaced by the darkness of night as he crawled into the crisp air that he could no longer feel, could no longer breathe. He did not mind that he could not enjoy the sensations of life, all he wanted was to perform the task given to him by Acantha so that he could be returned to the oblivion of death.

He climbed out of the rubble, stumbling over the fallen concrete until he reached an area away from the wreckage. Croom considered his appearance in the moonlight. He knew if he was to continue moving among the living to find Michael, he would at least need to resemble something human. At this moment his appearance wasn't even close.

The bolt shot into his chest had broken, but at least three inches of the wooden shaft still remained exposed. Croom grabbed the exposed shaft in a strong grip and pulled. The shaft finally jerked free with a ripping and tearing of long dead flesh. Dark decayed meat clung to the barbs on the head of the bolt. He examined the gaping hole left in his chest. Not able to smell the putrid odor wafting from the ravaged wound, he gave it no further thought.

His clothing would have to be replaced since they were ripped to shreds; his right boot was gone, buried in the collapsed building. A break-in at one of the merchant's shops in town that carried clothing would remedy the problem, and Croom would be ready to continue his pursuit.

It was a strange apparition that haunted the trail back towards the village that night. With his clothing torn, and covered head to foot in filth, Croom stalked through the same swirling fog, and on the same path that Michael and Sarah had followed just hours earlier.

Acantha came to him as he was in the deepest part of the hushed forest. With a force sufficient to knock the malignant man to his knees, she invaded his mind as she had earlier invaded his soul.

"Fool!" screamed the incensed voice in his head. "I sent you on a simple errand, and you failed."

"Not my fault." Croom panted from weakness as he knelt, head hanging, among the loam and fallen evergreen needles. "He called upon his magic and I was helpless to stand against it."

"Don't give me excuses! I saw through your eyes; you failed!" Acantha hissed.

From his kneeling position, Croom looked to the heavens. Whether beseeching Acantha or a greater power he had never known, was a question even he could not answer. "Give me rest, let me perish!" he cried.

"You will have your rest when you have done as instructed. Fail me, Croom, and I will see you walk the earth for eternity as a lost soul."

She left his mind then, and with a shudder he collapsed face first to the very earth she had taunted him with. Croom had no choice but to rise again to continue his hunt. He made his way through the fog-enshrouded, midnight forest with a matching blackness in his soul.

He was cautious as he entered the fallen city. He detested the necessity that brought him to the bounds of civilization; but was forced to take whatever steps were necessary to fulfill the task that Acantha's magic held him to.

He passed alone through the dead parts of the city – not caring about the rusted remains of the metal wagons, or the skeletons of the buildings of an earlier civilization that had captured Sarah's attention just hours earlier. He was too busy cursing everyone involved in this mess he was called upon to accomplish.

It was still a few hours before dawn when Croom entered a dark alley beside a shop that stocked hand-made clothing and leather goods. He fit in perfectly with the alley, a shadowy remnant of a man passing among the stinking refuse and garbage discarded by the shadier element of town. He was not much for stealth as he plodded across the urine-soaked dirt toward the side doorway, but there was no one about at this time of morning to note his passage. Reaching the doorway, he paused to listen for noises from inside that would tell of an early-rising shopkeeper. Hearing nothing, he pushed his shoulder and hip against the door just hard enough to break the latch without causing sufficient noise to raise alarm.

Fred Pitts had inherited the leather-makers shop about ten years earlier when his father was found beaten to death. The circumstances seemed to be suspicious by most of the town's inhabitants, but if the truth was to be told, not many would miss the abrasive elder Pitts. It was hoped that perhaps the younger Pitts would upgrade the shop and become a benefit to the town. Such was not to be the case.

He turned out to be an utterly unlikeable fellow. He was known for sloppy workmanship, cheating any customer slow-witted enough to be taken. And Pitts had a mean streak that landed him in the middle of the few brawls that he did not start himself. Thin and wiry he had built a good deal of strength in his hands and arms through his craft. He had unruly brown hair, a thin hollow face, and prominent yellow buck teeth. He kept a small room in the back of the shop for sleeping when he spent too much of his evening in one of the bars he constantly visited. On nights such as this, it was much easier to make it back to his shop than to try to find his way home.

Pitts was pulled from his sleep, still groggy, when the outer door was jarred open. It was the smell from Croom's wound that finally brought him fully awake. He sat up in bed, wondering what foul wind brought that stench to him, when he heard movement coming from the shop area. He padded barefoot over to the doorway connecting his little room with the shop. The two rooms were separated by a sheet of cloth hanging over the doorway. Pulling aside the cloth, Pitts peered into the adjoining room, squinting to make up for his poor eyesight.

Against the far wall to his right, he could see his leather-working tools hanging on pegs and scattered about his workbench. Dark-stained leather, his latest project, was being stretched near the bench.

All this was visible from the dim light that was let in through the broken door that opened into the alley. Looking out toward the center of the room were rough-finished tables with completed outfits: cotton and wool brought by the trading ships from the south, and his hand-made leather wear all mixed together, organized only by size groupings.

Hearing muffled noises and a dull thump, Pitts looked over into the farthest corner to his left in the front of the shop. Sitting on a short stool with his back turned was the man who had broken into his shop. He was a short burly figure, partly obscured by shadows, but Pitts could see he was putting on a new pair of leather boots that took many hours of hard labor to produce. This was not the first time his shop was broken into and he was robbed, but this fellow was not going to get away with it. Next to the bedroom doorway, only a few feet away, Pitts kept a four foot length of broken broom handle as an equalizer against any potentially unruly customers that might complain too vehemently about his shoddy workmanship.

Grabbing the length of solid wood in his right hand, he began sneaking up behind the unsuspecting thief. Wearing only baggy cotton undershorts he had put on three days earlier, he tip-toed closer, noticing the stench got stronger the nearer he got to the intruder.

"Take me a week to air the smell out of here once I get rid of this damn tramp," thought Pitts as he steadily moved closer to his target. Getting right up behind Croom, he raised the club high over his head.

"Time to pay your dues, you thief!" hollered Pitts as he brought the club down full force on Croom's head. His club broke in half, ricocheting off the wall and falling to the floor with a sharp clatter. The force of the blow cracked Croom's skull and caused his body to shudder under the impact.

Pitts stood frozen in place, mouth agape in shock, as the intruder stood and turned to face him. There was no pain, fear, or anger in the thief's eyes as expected, only cold dead indifference. The shopkeeper was rooted in terror as the unholy man took a step to reach him. Croom grabbed the shopkeeper by the throat with a vice-like grip and lifted him off the floor. Pitts knew there was no escape, no last minute pity from this man. Unlike his father, who had died at the hands of a violent and vengeful son, Pitts perished at the hands of a totally uncaring and unfeeling adversary.

*    *    *    *    *

As the sun finally began to peek over the inland hills, what appeared to be two fishermen and a boy steered their small yet sturdy boat toward the north. The rest of the small fishing fleet continued farther west towards the best fishing grounds, but Sarah, Michael and Oliver had a different goal this morning.

From the shore, a short thick man watched the boat making progress toward Cruz Town. He tried to push his dirty thinning hair down with short stubby fingers. He turned to begin the long walk north.

CHAPTER 6

Even though the few inhabitants of Cruz Town were used to seeing an occasional unkempt strange man coming down from the wild mountains east of town, they had never seen the likes of Big Thomas.

Well over six and a half feet tall, Big Thomas weighed more than three hundred pounds. As he strolled through the dusty streets of the small town there were few people about to notice, but the word spread quickly about the giant from the mountains.

The town folk that peeked around the shanty doors and other various hiding places were awed by the sight of this huge burly man. His dark curly hair had grown to shoulder-length and was matched by a wild beard that nearly reached his chest. He was dressed all in leather: boots, britches and vest. Darkly tanned massive arms sprouted from the vest like gnarled tree limbs.

The timid populace quit their hiding places when they realized this terrifying looking man was smiling and waving to them. Some of the braver towns-folk ventured a tentative wave in reply.

Thomas chuckled softly to himself about the reception he was receiving. It was the same reception he was given whenever he entered a town for the first time. It was a game to him by now, to see how long it would take the fearful to come out of hiding.

He had long since stopped trying to understand why people by nature believed that a man that looked like Thomas must naturally be violent or dangerous. While he had nothing against a good fracas now and again, Thomas had never been the instigator out of anger or meanness.

It was early morning when he first entered Cruz Town and most of the inhabitants were out on their boats fishing. From the shoreline he could see one boat slowly making its way to shore. It was too distant for him to see who was in the vessel or how many people there might be, so he made his way to the only tavern in the small town to wait for the arrival of the early returning fishing boat.

Thomas was finishing his second breakfast in the rundown shack that passed for a tavern when he saw three fishermen entering town from the old wooden dock area. This being the only logical destination in the small town, Thomas decided to wait.

He remained at his table by the window as he watched two men and a boy enter the nearly empty tavern. When the keeper of the tavern approached the three and led them to a table, Thomas nearly choked on his food as the supposed boy removed his hat and shook loose shoulder-length blonde hair. The transformation into a beautiful young woman was instant.

Perhaps he was wrong, the young man looked like the one he was told to bring back to Everett, but he had not been told about a beautiful young woman traveling with him. Still, if this was the man Everett wanted, this was the man Everett was going to get.

Michael was staring into space, once again cursing to himself for getting Sarah involved in this mess. He was startled back to reality when a large tanned face was thrust nose to nose with his. This large face was covered with black hair that opened into a wide grin. Michael continued to stare as the face pulled back from him until he could see it was attached to a mountain of a man with an overabundance of hair.

The huge man's face split into an even larger grin. "You got real green eyes, fella, so you must be the guy I'm looking for."

"W-what?" Michael stammered.

"Hey, what are you doing?" interjected Oliver. "We don't know you."

"Of course not," the large man replied as he drew up to his considerable full height. "I'm Big Thomas. A friend of mine asked me to come down here to meet this young man he knows from some time ago. He said the fella would be coming over from Monterey to find him. He described the fella just the way this one looks. See, right down to this big old ring he's wearing."

Thomas had reached down to grab Michael's hand in his own oversized fist, and was pointing to the large emerald ring he was wearing.

"My friend said it would be hard for me to see the ring, and danged if it ain't. I had to look real close to be sure it was there."

"You said a friend asked you to meet me. Who is your friend?" inquired Michael as he looked up at the man that held his hand in a firm yet gentle grasp.

"His name's Everett. A little old man, but I swear he does the strangest things. Says he's a magician if you can believe that." Thomas finally let Michael's hand fall from his own. "I think I believe him though. Like knowing you were going to be here today. How did he know that if he's not a magician?"

Michael let out a sigh of relief and looked over at Sarah. "Great, Everett is expecting us."

"Well, I don't know," mused Thomas. "He was sure expecting you by yourself, but he didn't say anything about this pretty woman. Come to think of it he didn't say anything about this other fella either."

"Perhaps not, but he won't mind a couple of visitors. Please, sit down with us Thomas, and I'll make introductions while we get something to eat. How about you, would you join us or have you already eaten?"

The big man smiled with satisfaction as he took a seat at the table. "Well, now that you mention it, I haven't had much to eat yet today."

\*　　\*　　\*　　\*　　\*

It was nearing noon when the four finally left the small village, bound for the low, yet roughly overgrown mountains beyond Cruz Town. Thomas led them to a rock outcropping outside town where he retrieved the pack of supplies he had brought on his short trip. The group then continued on toward the mountains where Everett had made his home for the past few weeks.

"Everett said you would be coming to him because of some trouble you're in. I've been sharing camp with him for the past couple of weeks, and have seen him do some pretty weird things. This time he did that meditating thing he does, and when he woke up he told me about you, and that you were coming. How does he do that?"

If Big Thomas lived most of his life in the wilds it was understandable that he would not be well informed about the art of magic.

"Everett was being truthful when he said he was a magician, Thomas," began Michael as they walked into the mountains. "He was my teacher at the magician's enclave, that's a few weeks travel south of here. I may not have been one of his best students, but there was no doubt that he was the best teacher."

"If he was such a good teacher," Sarah asked, a slight edge in her voice, "then why didn't you do any better?"

"Fair question," responded Michael. "As Everett will quickly point out, I just didn't care enough. It was all a game to me."

"Magicians almost destroyed the world," grumbled Oliver. "Was that a game, too?"

"Magicians are just like everyone else," responded Michael without a pause. "There were some evil men among the first magicians, and they had too much power."

"Go on, Michael," said Sarah. "You were telling us why you weren't one of Everett's best students."

"That's really all there is to it. Everett had infinite patience with me, but it never paid off for him. All I wanted to do was have fun. I'd sneak off from my studies every chance I got so that I could meet with my friends."

"Then there were other people at the enclave besides the magicians?" Sarah asked.

"Yes, but not many. The gardener had a couple of daughters that I was fond of."

"I don't think I want to hear about them," she responded with a frown.

Michael smiled. "Well, anyway, Everett could always find me. Whenever and wherever I would sneak off to, he would find me. It's like Thomas showing up to guide us. Everett knew when I was coming and where I would be."

"Is that a talent that Acantha has learned?" Oliver asked sternly.

Michael stopped smiling as he considered the possibilities. "I hope not, but probably."

"Who's Acantha?" asked Big Thomas.

Michael sighed and told him about the recent trouble at the magician's enclave. The day's travel was finally brought to a halt when Sarah began to show signs that she was tiring. She valiantly tried to keep up with Big Thomas' determined pace, but she had been through too much in the last twenty-four hours.

Michael had been keeping a concerned eye on her until he noticed she was falling further and further behind.

"Thomas, we need to stop. I must be worn out because of all I went through last night," he said.

"Oh, please Michael," panted Sarah. "You don't have to protect my image to Thomas and Oliver. They can see as well as you can that it's not you who is worn out, but me."

"Well, perhaps we're both ready to stop. How about it, Thomas, is there any place near here to rest for the night?"

"Sure," replied Thomas. "Just about a quarter-mile from here there's a clearing with a stream nearby. We can camp there. Everett didn't say I had to hurry."

In less than a half-hour they had stopped, and the men had gotten a cozy fire blazing with enough wood in the camp to last through the night. Sarah had stretched out near the fire using Thomas' empty pack for a pillow and was asleep before they could finish a meal of dried venison and spring water.

Michael spoke to Oliver as he looked at Sarah sleeping by the fire. "I have never asked Sarah how she came to be running a tavern. It didn't seem like an appropriate question."

"No mystery," responded Oliver quietly. "My best friend was her Uncle Gus. He started the tavern over thirty years ago, long before Sarah was born. Her parents died of a fever when she was only five years old. She had the same fever, and old Gus took her in and nursed her back to health. She has lived with him ever since.

"Gus died last year. Huntin' accident," Oliver continued, as he gazed into the fire. "Sarah stayed on in the tavern, not because it's the kind of life she wants, but because it's the only life she has ever known."

The three men were silent as they thought about the gentle young woman and the heartbreak she must have felt when she lost the last of her family.

"What about Charlie?" Michael asked softly.

"Ah, Charlie," Oliver responded with a smile. "You know, the seamen that came into port in Monterey all eventually wind up at old Gus's tavern. Once they were there, some of these gruff men couldn't help but make advances at Gus's beautiful niece. Old Gus would toss them out the front door where they would land face-down in the dusty street outside.

"The word was eventually spread not to tamper with Gus's niece. When Charlie showed up he was instantly smitten with Sarah. Naturally he found himself rolling in the dust outside. What separated Charlie from the rest of the riffraff was that he was enchanted with Sarah in an innocent way. He's a bit simple, you know. And then his integrity was shown when he picked himself up from the dust and re-entered the tavern to apologize to Gus and Sarah.

"After that, he remained in Monterey to work the fishing boats. When Gus died, Sarah gave him work. Charlie eventually became capable enough to be left in charge of the bar at night, freeing Sarah from the long hours she had been working."

"Sounds like a real good man," offered Thomas. "I hope I'm lucky enough to meet him someday."

"I hope you do too," answered Oliver. "But right now I think I'm going to do like Sarah and get some sleep."

Michael stayed awake into the night as those around him slept. He was lost in thought about Sarah and the life she had led. He felt even closer to her now that he knew of some of the hardships that she had had to endure.

*     *     *     *     *

While Michael's group was relaxing, Acantha was railing in her keep. The former magician's enclave, now Acantha's keep, took on the appearance of a mystical castle as the sun shone its last rays of the day on the towers. In her laboratory, in the highest part of the castle, she stalked across the floor to the far wall, only to turn about and stalk back.

"They're still trying to stop me," she yelled at one of the simple men she kept as an enslaved servant.

The hapless flunky ducked and cringed as she grabbed a nearby foul-smelling flask and hurled it at him. If only she would immerse herself in her scheming and planning again, then maybe he could escape the room unseen. Perhaps another luckless soul would suffer her next tirade, but he would be free until it was his turn to be called again.

"You!" she screamed, pointing a dagger-like finger at the cowering man. "What are you staring at?"

"Nothing Mistress, I swear it! Nothing!"

"Get out of my sight! You disgust me, cowering there like an idiot. Must I do everything myself?"

"Yes, Mistress. I mean, no, Mistress. I mean, I'm leaving, Mistress."

The fortunate man turned on his heels and fled the room before the enraged woman could change her mind. When the offending man was finally gone, Acantha sat at her workbench and with a sweep of her hand angrily brushed the multi-colored beakers half-filled with fluids, paperwork, jars laden with dust, and various roots, herbs and dried animal parts to the floor.

She leaned over one of the few remaining items on her bench. It was a large shallow-bottom crystal bowl. It was filled to the brim with fresh dark-red blood. It had taken her most of the day to draw this much blood from two of her servants without killing them. They were needed too much to perform the mundane tasks around the castle for her to kill them needlessly.

Slowly she passed one hand over the bowl repeatedly. On that hand was the ruby ring. As she passed her hand over the ornate crystal bowl, the richly colored blood began to clear. As it cleared, the ruby grew even darker red than before. She could see them now, Michael sitting on a wooded hillside next to a campfire. Asleep next to him was the girl she had seen in her bowl two months earlier. Now two others were added to the scene, an old weather-beaten man, and a huge man covered with hair.

No matter, she knew where he was again. It was the same area she had seen when she had spied on Everett, the old man that had warned Michael in the first place. If he was going to Everett, it pleased her greatly. She could be rid of them both at the same time. She would need to contact Croom. Once he was on his way to where they were hiding, she could relax for a while. When he finally reached them, she would be ready for battle. This time there would be no mistakes. This time she would control Croom's every movement. It would be she who would stop the meddlesome old man and Michael.

With a wave of her hand, the scene in the bowl changed from the wooded hillside to the beaches just north of Monterey. Along this darkening beach walked a short man in new leather boots and coat. Although the clothing was new, Croom's appearance had deteriorated. The stench followed him wherever he went. Acantha could see in her ensorcelled bowl that he would not be able to pass among the living any longer.

"You are a mess, Croom."

He stopped his plodding steps and looked around. "You invade my mind again, Acantha."

"You have no mind, Croom."

"What do you want of me now? Have I not suffered enough?"

"I am not concerned with your suffering! Fail me and you will suffer forever!"

"What must I do? Tell me so I can do it and finish this walking hell!"

"Michael is in the mountains in the north. He is going to that old teacher of his, Everett. I want you to go there and finish what I had you begin months ago. I want them both dead! I want that ring!"

Croom turned to look towards the mountains. It would be about a three-day walk just to approach the beginnings of the mountains. No matter, he had all the time in the world.

Acantha peered deeper into the bowl. "Croom," she hissed. Croom jerked as though struck. "Again, I warn you...Don't fail me!"

Acantha once again waved her hand over the crystal. Her ring had absorbed all of the life-giving force of the blood, and now it was just a pool of clear lifeless fluid. She grasped the now useless bowl in her hands as she went to the window to dump the contents.

"Your future, Michael," she whispered to herself as she tossed the contents from the window. "Yours and the old man's. Just dead, useless garbage."

CHAPTER 7

Michael and Sarah woke at the same time to the delicious aroma of meat cooking on an open fire. When the sleep finally left their eyes, they saw Thomas and Oliver tending to what was to be their morning meal over the campfire.

Oliver turned as he became aware of them. "About time you pups woke up," he remarked. "I told you two I could keep up with you. Seems I'm doing better than that."

"What is that wonderful smell?" asked Sarah as they approached the fire.

"Roast pig," answered Thomas as he busied himself over the cook fire. "How about some ham steaks for breakfast?"

Michael braced the small of his back with both hands as he bent backward to stretch the kinks loose from sleeping on the ground. He deeply inhaled the damp, early morning air. "I give up, how did you manage roast pig for breakfast?" he asked.

"I live in the mountains, Michael, I can't just go to the nearest tavern for my meals. You live in the wilds like this, you learn to fend for yourself. Oliver and I got up early and tracked for game. Didn't take me long to find this fella. One flex of the bow, and we have breakfast. Oliver helped me lug it back here so that you two sleepy heads could feed your faces."

"Well," Michael said with a chuckle, "it's lucky we have the two of you with us. I don't think either of us thought ahead to our next meal."

The four enjoyed ample fare of ham steaks and mushrooms, washing it down with fresh spring water that Oliver had taken from the stream.

Sarah was enjoying what was a totally new experience for her. She had never slept under the stars before, let alone waking to the smell of wild boar roasting on an open fire.

She did not give much thought to the danger that had so recently passed. She felt quite secure with these capable men. She put her problems behind her, and enjoyed licking the flavorful grease from her fingers.

The morning hunt seemed to help bring the old fisherman and the mountain man closer together, as they were deep in animated conversation while eating. Thomas was living up to the needs of his girth by consuming as much of the roast pig as did his three companions put together.

Of the travelers, only Michael was deep in thought about what had happened two nights earlier. His main concern was the future. He was sure Everett could help, but Everett wanted to return for the ruby ring. Michael fervently hoped the old magician would help them escape, and not try to persuade him to join in the quest for the ruby. He wanted no part of any quest; he only wanted a normal life. As they doused the fire, being sure it was totally out to avoid what could become a devastating wildfire, Thomas explained to them what to expect next on their trip through the mountains.

"We'll head east from here toward that summit over there," he said as he pointed to their destination.

"Before we get there, a couple of hours from now in fact, we'll meet up with the weed people. They'll capture us and take us to their camp. We'll stay there for the night."

"Weed people? Capture us?" exclaimed a startled Sarah. "What do you mean we're going to be captured by weed people? Michael, what's he talking about?"

Michael seemed as puzzled as Sarah over who, or what, the weed people were.

"I don't know," responded Michael. "Who are the weed people, Thomas?"

"Oh, sorry," said Thomas with an embarrassed grin. "Not being mountain folk you probably don't know about the weed people. Let's get on our way and I'll explain."

The four travelers began their early morning trek farther into the lush green mountains. Although the going was rough in places, the fresh spring air helped to invigorate them as they walked.

There were places along the way that showed the mark of the mysterious past society shown in Michael's books. One moment they would be pushing their way through heavy undergrowth, the next they would break free into a clearing where the ground would be covered with the broken concrete Sarah was so used to seeing in the village.

Even out here in the wild, she thought. They must have been able to go anywhere with ease.

As she was thinking of these past people, she was also listening to Thomas' explanation of the weed people.

"The weed people are a tribe of mountain folk. Totally harmless, but don't tell them that. They try very hard to be a fierce lot. They're just so fumbling and ineffective that they are hard to take seriously. They're called weed people because they smoke weeds that they grow up here in the mountains. The stuff really addles their brains though. Just smoke this stuff of theirs a few times and it does strange things to your mind...and they smoke it all the time."

"Is that what makes them so fumbling?" asked Sarah as she struggled to keep up with Thomas' steady gait.

"Yeah, it's like that stuff has fried their brains. They have always used it. Their parents used it and their parent's parents. They get forgetful at times, so they may forget to bring us back to their camp once they capture us, so we have to be ready to remind them."

"I must be missing something here, Thomas," Oliver interjected. "Why do we want these weed people to capture us?"

Big Thomas threw his massive arms out to the side in a gesture of helplessness. "It's that Everett. He does some strange things. Actually, he just likes these people. They think he's some kind of prophet or something. So, the weed people capture us. Then they'll send someone to Everett telling him about the four people they caught trying to reach him. This way they get to feel useful to him. He says it gives them purpose, if you get what I mean."

"I'm not sure I do," Oliver muttered to himself.

"It sounds as though you're pretty fond of Everett," said Michael. "Do you do everything he asks of you?"

Thomas stopped his steady pursuit of the summit. The stop was greatly appreciated by Sarah. Although they had been traveling just a little over an hour, the steady uphill grade and Thomas' mile-grinding pace was taking its toll.

She took the opportunity to pull off the unfamiliar boots Oliver had found for her. They had last been used by a boy from the village who would occasionally help him on his fishing boat. She began rubbing her tired feet, enjoying the relief as Thomas answered Michael's question:

"Yeah, I reckon I'd do just about anything that little old man wanted me to. He saved my life you know. That's how we met."

"What happened?" asked Sarah as she looked up at the large man from her seat on a fallen tree.

Thomas sat next to her on the log, giving the cue to all that they could take a few minutes for rest.

"Well, it's a bit embarrassing to me," he answered sheepishly. "After all, I live in these mountains. I'm supposed to be in control all the time; but I guess everyone slips up once in a while. It's just if you slip up too badly here, it can get you killed.

"I was hunting in an area I should not have been in. There had been a mama bear and a couple of her cubs reported in the area by some of the other mountain folk. Believe me, if you see a couple of bear cubs, head in the opposite direction, 'cause if the mama's nearby she won't be happy to see you."

Sarah began scanning the surrounding woods. Oliver could not help smiling at the wide eyes of the innocent young woman.

"I damn near bumped into that bear," Thomas continued. "She had to have been over eight feet tall. Boy, was she pissed to see me; ah...sorry, ma'am," he added for Sarah's sake.

"She roared, and swatted at me. Like to caved in my chest. Next thing I know I'm flat on my back with this raging beast standing over me. She was roaring, and clawing at the air, muscles rippling as if she was fighting the air to get at me. I was so frightened, that it took me nearly a minute to realize she wasn't coming any closer. Just clawing at the air and roaring, but she wasn't moving.

"Pretty soon this little roly-poly fella comes trotting over to me. 'You all right?' he asked me. Now mind you this eight foot bear is standing over me screaming at the wind, and here's this little bitty fella leaned over with his hands on his knees, looking at me, asking if I was all right!"

"So...this little guy put a hex or something on the bear. Is that right, Thomas?" asked Oliver thoughtfully.

"Yeah, I guess that's what he did. At least he did something, or I wouldn't be here talking about it."

The tale told, a few minutes later the group continued deeper into the Cruz Mountains to find the roly-poly Everett. Oliver did not join in the friendly banter. He remained silent, deep in thought.

Perhaps all of this time he had been wrong about magicians, Oliver thought. One tends to grow up learning prejudices from those around them. In retrospect he could not remember ever having met a magician personally, except Michael. He had been quite fond of the boy, until he had learned of his past.

The stories he was now hearing about Everett just did not match with the previous opinion of magicians that had been induced by fear and prejudice. He sounded like a kind, gentle man.

"So what happened to the bear, Thomas?" Oliver finally asked.

"What bear?" replied Thomas. He was confused by the return to the earlier subject.

"You know, the bear that attacked you. The one Everett put a hex on."

"Oh...nothing."

"What do you mean nothing? He must have done something with the bear. Did he kill it? Did he make it disappear...what?"

"No, nothing like that," replied Thomas with a shrug. "He helped me away from the area. I don't know how he did that either, considering the size of me. Then when we were far enough away, the bear lurched forward as if some invisible hand that was holding her was taken away. She went back to her cubs and away they went."

The next hour of traveling was done in silence, though the shared thought was that they were all thankful the old magician had spared the life of the mother bear.

Finally Thomas called a halt.

"Do you hear that?" he asked.

"What?" replied Michael, instantly alert. "I don't hear anything."

"Quiet, and listen," Thomas ordered.

As they all stood still, the normal forest sounds began to lessen. Eventually human sounds began to reach them.

Oliver was the first to speak. "It sounds like someone is giggling."

Sarah looked over to Michael with her brows knitted together as though in question.

"What is it, Thomas?" he asked.

"Weed people, I think. This is their territory."

As Sarah began to look around her, trying to see into the dense woods, and lush undergrowth, Thomas saw her apprehension.

"Now don't worry, Sarah. Believe me when I tell you they aren't dangerous. They think they are, but they are as far from dangerous as you can get. Just go along with them."

Sarah did not feel reassured as she stood waiting to be captured by a group of mountain folk called the weed people. As they waited, the noise level of the marauding band of men became more raucous. The noise was quite often punctuated by uncontrolled giggling.

Beyond the dense greenery, a strange assortment of men was approaching. Every one of them was as thin and underfed as Thomas was large and overfed. All were covered with long tangled, dirty hair and beards. Their clothing was rags.

The men carried their most prized possessions – a small bone pipe held by a leather strap hanging around their filthy necks. Although small, the pipes were crafted with care, depicting hand-carved scenes of the forest. Most of the pipes were handed down from generation to generation as a family heirloom. Contrary to the condition of the weed people themselves, the small bone pipes were obviously cared for reverently.

Some of the men were actively smoking the weed-packed pipes as they clumped through the forest. The result was thirty pairs of glazed eyes.

"Hey, shut up, you guys," came the admonishment after one burst of prolonged giggling. "They be not much further. We needs to scare them. Giggling won't do no scarin'."

"Okay?" demanded the evident leader. "Now we be splitting up, and circling round-abouts them. As we be circling, we be chanting."

Nearly thirty seconds passed before the leader erupted at his fellow weed smokers. "Well, what are you standing here looking at me for? Spread out!"

His orders were answered by spurts of laughter and giggling. Along with the laughter was a chorus of, "Sshh! Sshh! Quiet, they'll hear us." Almost immediately the chanting began:

*"Tokin,' tokin,' we been-a-smokin'*

*Come 'round here and you'll get broken.*

*Tokin,' tokin,' we ain't-a-jokin'*

*Get outa here and don't be pokin'.*

*Tokin,' tokin,' we been-a-smokin'*

*So leave right now cause we have spoken.*

The chant always ended with sounds of laughter that followed the ever-expanding circle that was moving around Michael's group. The chanting ended when the circle was completed amid suppressed laughter. All was silent for scant seconds before the leader yelled, "Now, CHARGE!"

Sarah stared in disbelief as a skinny, ill-kept man dressed in rags, came charging out of the cover of the woods. The wild man who was the leader was covered in more hair than even Thomas was able to match, and he looked as though he had not washed in months.

He raced out of the woods at the group standing in the clearing. Shaking his fist and glowering, he rushed toward his intended prisoners. His charge slowed as he neared them and then he came to a complete stop. The fierce expression on his face changed to perplexity as he looked around him.

The brush surrounding the clearing remained undisturbed and swayed gently in the afternoon breeze. He had rushed to the attack completely alone.

He turned to gape one last time at the group of travelers, and with a crestfallen look on his face, turned and raced back to the woods.

In a state of near panic, he crashed through a tangle of bushes and vines to return to the relative safety of concealment.

Upon reaching the far side of the wall of brush bordering the clearing, he fell to his hands and knees to catch his failing breath.

Attempting to regain his composure, he glared in all directions, searching for his hidden comrades.

"All right you guys!" yelled the begrimed leader. "Why didn't you follow me? I said 'charge,' and you're supposed to charge when I say 'charge'!"

Amid more laughter, one of the band could be heard calling back to his leader, "What happened, Toby? You go out there and round them up yourself, did you?"

Oliver stared at where the disheveled man had disappeared into the woods. While he was trying to comprehend the failed attack, the leader of the weed people was the target of nearly two minutes of cat-calls and jeers from his friends.

"I don't believe it, Thomas," he was finally able to say. "They're much more ridiculous than you said. They're absolutely unbelievable!"

"Yeah. I knew you would all stop worrying as soon as you saw them. I figured seeing is believing."

Inside the cover of the woods the leader of the weed people was still trying to organize the attack.

"Now we're gonna try this again. I'll be yelling 'charge' and when I do, you'll all be charging. Now get ready."

Once again the forest became still.

"CHARGE!"

From the forest ran thirty raggedly-dressed men. The woods were filled with the cacophony of the yelling, laughing, and giggling men.

The leader of the group chose at that moment to trip over an exposed root. He fell yelling and screaming to the ground, with leaves, dirt, and the torn rags of his clothing flying in all directions.

What little organization was achieved among the attackers collapsed into joyous disorder. Some of the men rolled on the ground, holding their sides as they laughed at their leader's misfortune. Most ignored Michael and his friends as they rushed to their fallen leader.

"Hey, Toby," giggled the first to reach him, "what you be doing on the ground? You trying to fly, were you?"

Soon the entire invading force surrounded the hapless Toby as they tried to help him. After they had helped him to his feet, and all had thanked him for giving them such an amusing afternoon, they turned to leave.

"Michael, I think they have forgotten us," said a disbelieving Sarah.

"I think you're right," Michael answered as he watched the backs of the retreating force.

"I was afraid this might happen," said Thomas. "We'll just have to help them. Hey, you guys!" he yelled at the weed people before they could reach the edge of the clearing. "Don't hurt us! We'll come quietly."

Toby turned around as though Michael's group had snuck up on them. "There they are!" He rushed towards them as his supporters followed.

"Don't try to escape!" he yelled as he approached the four travelers. "We got weapons. We'll use 'em if we have to."

He turned to the nearest grimy weed smoker as he realized he did not have his weapon.

"Hey, Pot-Face, who brought the clubs?"

"I don't know, Toby, I thought you brought them."

"Right, thirty clubs! You think I'm carrying thirty clubs! That stuff you're smoking is going to your brain, boy."

Thomas could see this was getting them nowhere, and his patience was beginning to slip.

"You don't need any weapons, fellas. We can see we're badly outnumbered. Michael, Sarah, Oliver, put your hands up, these guys captured us fair and square."

Sarah looked over at Michael; eyes asking the question she did not give voice to. Michael shrugged his shoulders, as confused as she was, but raised his hands anyway.

Eventually the weed people were capable of tying the hands of the captives behind their backs. The one called Pot-Face was selected to bind Sarah's hands.

"I be sorry 'bout tying you up and all, girlie, but we warned you to be gone when we was chantin'," admonished the skinny man. His voice softened. "Now, you be tellin' me if these ropes be too tight. Don't want to hurt you none. Just don't tell Toby that I be concerned 'bout you."

"No," Sarah replied to the man, "you're not hurting me." She looked to her captor with a friendly smile, which immediately caused his face to become scarlet red. He promptly covered his flushed face with his hands.

"Hey, Pot-Face," called Toby, "how you goin' to watch her if you got your face covered up?"

"Sorry, Toby," he replied. "Must have gotten something in my eye."

"Right! Let's go, then. Move 'em out to camp!"

It was not long after they began marching through the deep woods when Sarah noticed a problem beginning with her bonds.

"Michael," she whispered. "I think the rope they tied my hands with is coming undone."

"I'm not surprised," he replied. "Mine has already come loose. Just catch it in your hands when it does, and hold it. As wasted as these people are, I doubt they'll ever notice."

It was a short trip to the weed people's camp. As they reached the boundaries of the camp, their captors once again forgot them as all thirty of the men ran shouting to their women about their brave deed. Michael and his friends were left standing on the outskirts of the makeshift village.

"What do we do now?" asked Oliver.

"We just go into the camp, and remind Toby to send a runner to Everett," replied Thomas.

Sarah stared around her at the squalor of the camp, as if the suggestion to enter might be avoided.

All about the large clearing were makeshift lean-tos and huts, in varying degrees of disrepair. In the center of the camp were a number of rough wooden tables with the leaves of their cherished weeds drying in the sun.

The women of the camp dropped what they were doing to rush to their returning men. Some of the women had been tending to the leaves drying in the sun; others were working the strong fibers into hemp rope.

It was some time before Thomas was able to attract Toby's attention to send a runner to Everett. Toby seemed not to notice that the prisoners' hands were no longer tied.

"Right!" Toby replied. "I'll send someone to see the miracle-man, and you will all be our guests tonight. There will be singing and dancing around the campfire in your honor."

To Sarah's relief, it appeared they had changed from prisoners to honored guests.

By the time the sun had fully set, the celebration was in full swing. Toby and his men had built a large bonfire, capable of providing warmth for all the men and women of the camp, as well as their prisoners turned guests.

Along with two members of the camp, Thomas and Oliver took a short hunting trip that was rewarded with a full-size stag. That, plus the food supplies the weed people maintained, furnished a meal fit to the occasion.

After eating, Sarah rested in Michael's arms and watched the roaring fire. The camp members, men and women both, danced wildly around the fire. The music was a simple rhythm produced by beating clubs against hollow logs.

The weed people used any occasion other than normal everyday activities as a reason to have a celebration. They were very practiced in the art of celebrating. This was evident by the joyous, uninhibited dancing, and the stirring beat of the music.

Sarah was given only a brief time to relax before the giggling Pot-Face ran up to her.

"Come on, Sarah! Dance around the fire with me."

"I'm afraid I wouldn't know how to dance around a campfire, Pot-Face," she replied with a laugh.

"Come on, I'll show you." The persistent man was pulling her to her feet as everyone teased her.

As Sarah attempted to match the dance pattern shown by her partner, she noticed Oliver had already been included in the festivities. He was truly jubilant as he cavorted around the fire with a woman a third his age.

"This is wonderful fun, Sarah," he shouted. "You should get into trouble more often."

Thomas moved over to sit on the ground beside Michael. Relaxed, the two men watched their companions dancing in laughter around the fire.

"Oliver seems to be enjoying himself," the big man offered. "That's good, he was awfully tense when I first met you three."

"Well, with good reason, I'm afraid," Michael replied.

"Yeah, I know. He said he was never fond of magicians to begin with, and then he finds out you're one. I think his opinion is softening a bit though. He has learned that you're truly a good man."

Thomas gave Michael an appraising look before continuing. "You haven't learned to live up to what you gotta do yet, but we both feel you will."

Michael was startled, and jerked his head to return the mountain-man's look.

"You two seem to have become confidants."

"We hunt together," replied Thomas, as though that was explanation enough.

"As far as not living up to my obligations is concerned," Michael continued, as he looked back at the festivities, "there is more to the situation than you are aware of."

Thomas rose from the ground and stretched, with arms wide. "Doesn't matter. I just feel you'll do what's needed. Now it's to bed for me, we'll probably get an early start in the morning."

Michael watched the back of the retreating giant as he considered their brief conversation. He wondered why everyone wanted him to do what he was set against. Why could he not just be left alone?

As he sat there, lost in thought, Sarah returned from the wild dance around the fire. She expelled a great sigh as she fell into his arms.

"I'm exhausted, Michael." She wiped away the perspiration that had beaded on her forehead in spite of the brisk night air. "I think I needed this festive night. I feel so much better now."

He returned her smile with one of his own. "We had better call it a night. Thomas said it would probably be an early start tomorrow. Toby has given us the use of one of the huts for tonight. We'll just go chase the vermin out, then retire for the night."

At Sarah's shocked expression, he relented. "No, no...I was just teasing you. There are no vermin, I swear it. You will sleep safe and sound tonight."

"Not too soundly, I hope," Sarah interrupted as she peered into the eyes of the man she loved.

CHAPTER 8

The runner returned to camp just after dawn the next morning. He rushed to Toby's lean-to with instructions from the miracleman. The four strangers were to be sent to him straight-away.

Michael and Sarah were awakened when Pot-Face came running into their hut. When he saw Sarah was still in bed he promptly covered his face with his hands.

"I'm sorry I came in here like this," he said through the covering of his hands. "But Toby says you'll be going now. So, you'll have to get up now, 'cause Toby says so."

Upon delivering his message, without waiting for a response, Pot-Face turned to flee the embarrassing situation. Unfortunately, he failed to uncover his eyes before racing from the room. With a substantial thud, he ran full speed into the wooden frame for the door. He hit the floor, and lay sprawled on his back, with a cloud of dust floating up to cover him.

"It would appear you have an admirer, Sarah," said Michael, as he watched the dust settle over the fallen man.

"Don't you think we should help him? He's out cold."

"He'll be all right. Let's go see what Toby wants."

Outside, near the now-cold campfire, Thomas and Oliver were waiting. They had been up when the runner had returned from Everett. Thomas' pack was fully loaded, and the two men were ready to travel.

"Get the sleep out of your eyes, kids," called Oliver as they approached. "It's time to travel."

"What about breakfast?" replied Sarah as they approached.

"We've got cold venison and bread," Thomas answered. "We'll eat on the way. We should be with Everett in about two hours."

The four said their good-byes to the weed-people. Even Pot-Face had managed to show up for their departure. The knot above his left eye was gaining prominence as they wished each other well.

Two hours later, the four were nearing the summit that Thomas had pointed out the morning before. The travel was easier here; the forest was thinning out, as well as the underbrush. The hillside was lush with the thick golden grass of summer. Several large oak trees were at the top of the hill where Everett kept his camp. As they reached the campsite, there was sufficient evidence that someone was staying there, but there was no sign of Everett. The four looked around the camp for clues that might tell them in which direction he may have gone.

"I thought he would be here, waiting," said Thomas as he looked around the clearing.

"Maybe he is out hunting somewhere," offered Oliver.

"I don't hunt, young man," came a disembodied voice.

Everyone began turning in all directions to find the source of the voice. All except Michael.

"Hello, my old friend," he said. "It is very good to see you again."

Sarah, Oliver, and Thomas turned to look at Michael as though he had lost his senses, and was speaking to the air. They saw that he was looking up. Following his example, they turned their gazes upward, toward the top of the nearest oak tree. There, floating gently among the upper-most branches, was the aged magician.

He sat in the air with his legs crossed, hands folded into his lap, as if he were resting on solid ground. His plain brown robe constantly tugged at him as the wind swirled softly around the master. He was indeed a roly-poly little man, barely reaching five feet in height. He must have been nearly eighty years old, if appearance could be trusted. What sparse gray hair he had left was flowing loosely in the gentle wind.

"Good Lord, I've never seen him do anything like that before!"

"I meant to spare you the fear everyone feels toward magicians, my large gentle friend." Everett spoke to Thomas as he slowly floated to the ground from his perch in the air.

As he settled to the earth he spoke to everyone. "I believe now, however, that the time to hide magical abilities has come to an end. We face a great challenge, and the only chance we have is magic."

Once on firm footing he turned to Sarah. "Even more important to this old world is beautiful women. You must be Sarah."

She stood there in stunned silence, as though her feet had taken root. Her mouth open in surprise.

"Perhaps I have rushed things a bit," Everett continued as he turned to Michael. "Would you be so kind as to offer introduction, Michael?"

Little response was given to the introductions that were made.

"Please, please," implored the old master. "We have many things to discuss, and it would be so much easier if more than one person was capable of speech."

"Right," Oliver managed, nodding toward Sarah. "Forgive us, we have never been exposed to magic in any aspect, let alone being approached by a man floating in the air."

"I've never seen you do anything like that either," said Thomas, his voice redolent with astonishment.

"I'm sorry," Sarah put in. "I'm pleased to meet a friend of Michael's."

It seemed that once the dam of surprise was broken, the questions and comments came in a torrent. All began to speak at once. Michael and Everett were able to stem the tide of conversation just long enough to move to the center of Everett's camp where they could continue in relative comfort.

It was past noon by the time they had settled in comfortably, and talked about the attack on Michael and Sarah, as well as the two-day trip into the mountains.

"Well, it seems you have all had a very busy couple of days. In light of what I have heard, Michael and I need to come to some conclusions. However, there is information that directly involves Michael, which he is not aware of as yet. If the three of you would be so kind as to prepare a bit of lunch, I would like to take a stroll with my young magician."

Once Everett had steered him from the camp, Michael was quick to object.

"I know what you are doing, you tricky old man. You're going to try to convince me to join you in getting the ruby back from Acantha. I've already told you I'm not interested. As long as I have the emerald, her power is limited. I'm willing to keep it, and make sure she doesn't take it. That's all!"

"Oh, Michael! Surely you have more intelligence than that. Surely I have taught you better. Do you really believe she will allow you to go your own way unmolested? She wants that ring, and she will stop at nothing to regain it."

Michael's lips were compressed into a slash of a straight line, his jaw jutting outward in defiance.

"It's a terrible thing I have to do now, Michael, but I see there is no other way."

Everett sat on the hillside, and overlooked the high rolling hills that passed for mountains in this part of the country. He indicated Michael should join him. When they were both sitting, and Everett decided his friend had calmed down sufficiently, he began to give him a history lesson.

"You have asked me before why I gave the emerald ring to you to protect," he began. "You were at least astute enough to realize that it was odd for the lesser talent to be entrusted with such power. I refrained from a more detailed explanation at the time simply because you were not ready for it. You must know the truth now, whether you are ready for it or not."

Michael pulled his gaze from the beauty of the deeply-wooded mountains to study his old friend.

"You sound ominous, old man. You taught me as well as possible at the enclave, and I learned much from you. What could you have possibly been able to hide from me that would cause such strain?"

"The sins of their fathers," muttered Everett to himself.

"What?"

"Nothing. Nothing." Everett waved his hand in the air as if to dispel his last statement. He looked back kindly at Michael. The two had been friends even before Michael was old enough to speak his first words. The old magician was deeply saddened that he would be the instrument of his young friend's pain.

"I really must learn to dispense with these dramatics. Michael, the reason Acantha is so strong with the ruby, and why you could be so strong with the emerald, is because of who you are.

"If anyone else controlled either of those rings, or both, the enhancement of their power would be negligible. Only someone of your bloodline can call on the powers of the two rings."

Michael was quiet while he considered the information just given to him by his teacher. He could understand what he was being told, but there was something that did not fit. There was some reason why what Everett told him could not be true. He had it, he knew what was wrong.

"That can't be right, Everett. There must be others that can call on the talismans. Remember, it was you that taught me that these same stones were used in the Magicians' War. There was a magician back then that used the stones in concert. That was one of the acts that nearly destroyed all of mankind."

"Precisely," said Everett quietly.

Michael jumped to his feet. His face was deathly white, as if all the blood had run out of him. He staggered and nearly fell under the weight of this terrible knowledge.

"No!" he yelled. "No. Not one of my ancestors. It wasn't one of my ancestors that did that!"

"It's true, Michael. I'm sorry it had to be told to you this way. But think, lad, why of all the places in the world these stones could be found, why are they here? Why are they here, in the same place you are? Your parents knew the truth. That's why they were at the enclave. They died before you were even old enough to know them, but like the other descendants of the terrible man that did this, they vowed to protect the world from it ever happening again. Now it is your turn!"

"Destroy the rings!" Michael shouted. "Destroy them now, and it will never happen again!"

"That's been tried, my young friend. They cannot be destroyed. No power has been found that could do it. Now, perhaps, you can see why you must come back with me. Why it must be you. Only you can call on the powers of the emerald. Only you can regain the ruby from Acantha, now that it is holding her so firmly. Only you can awaken the emerald."

"No! No!" Michael cried. He was nearly pulling his hair out in his struggle to accept the blame for his ancestor's dark deeds. Yet another guilt to carry. "I don't believe it," he wailed as he ran down the hill.

"Ah, my young friend," Everett whispered to himself, "such a burden for you to carry. Such a burden...It's not fair, but no one can carry it for you. If only I could!"

$$* \quad * \quad * \quad * \quad *$$

Many miles to the south, Acantha was once again bent over her nefarious bowl. She had watched Michael's progress through the Cruz Mountains closely.

She had witnessed the attack by the weed people as it happened. At first she had hoped this wild-looking group would solve her problems. It soon became evident that she was viewing a farce. This ludicrous gathering of human refuse was incapable of sustaining thought, let alone maintaining a concerted effort. Michael and his group had reached Everett; that pious little gnome showing off with his meager powers!

"You have given knowledge to me as well, I must admit. Not just anyone could do what I plan. I was chosen. The power is my natural destiny. You have no right to try to take it from me!"

She watched as Everett made his way back up the hill toward Michael's friends. She felt he may succeed in recruiting Michael, with this latest gambit.

"No matter, old fool," Acantha continued to herself. "Croom is on his way, and you will be dealt with!"

Everett halted nearly in mid-stride. He raised and cocked his head at an angle as though he were listening for an elusive sound.

With a shudder, he shook his head and continued to his camp.

CHAPTER 9

Michael was unaware of where he was running. He was just trying to run away from the truth. Of course it was true. All of it was true. He had been around magic long enough to know that what Everett had told him was more than just possible, it was probable. A talisman that could channel power for one person was quite often completely dead to the touch of others.

Perhaps deep down, he had touched upon the possibilities of the enchanted stones being keyed in only to Acantha and himself. Why else would have Everett given him the stone, rather than keeping it himself? Everett's greater power enhanced by the emerald would have been enough to defeat Acantha.

He could have figured that out weeks ago, if he had let himself. But, he wouldn't. So, he had run. For weeks he had been running. Now he had Sarah. He had thought he could just settle in a sleepy little village, ignore all of his problems and maybe they would go away. They wouldn't.

Now Sarah. What about her? He truly loved her and would die trying to protect her if that's what it took. But to go back and look the prospect of that death in the face....

Could he just go on running? He was putting Sarah in danger by allowing Acantha to pursue him unchecked. He was sure Acantha could find them no matter where they went, and he would not only have to protect himself, but Sarah as well. She had no talent that would save her life. She was a beautiful girl, perfect in every way; but she was not a fighter.

He brooded for hours as he walked morosely through the forest. He was lost in thought and failed to notice the beauty of his surroundings. The sky was beginning to darken when he finally reached his decision and began to make his way back to Everett's camp.

Sarah leaped to her feet as Michael came into the light of the fire. He was exhausted and emotionally drained. "Michael, you've been gone so long! I was worried about you."

He smiled as he moved into an embrace with her. "You need not have worried, Everett is able to sense me within certain distances. If I had been in trouble, he would have known about it immediately. But I appreciate the fact that you worry about me."

"You have made a decision, haven't you?" she asked.

"Yes. Everett has convinced me. Acantha's threat must be dealt with. He and I will be going south in the next couple of days."

He could not bring himself to tell Sarah the reasons behind his sudden change of mind. There was too much guilt involved to tell her about his ancestor that had destroyed a civilization, and had nearly destroyed mankind. Too much shame.

"Wonderful news, Michael," interrupted Everett as he approached. "I knew when the time came you would make the right decision. There is really no other recourse, you know."

"No, wait just a minute!" flared Sarah. "I don't want you to go away. I don't want you going into that danger. What about us? What about our plans?"

"That's just the point, Sarah, if I don't go to the trouble, it will come to me. As long as that's true, we won't have the chance to live out our plans.

"Besides," he added, "I won't be going alone, Everett is coming with me, and he will be able to teach me how to control the power of the emerald." At least I hope he will, he thought to himself.

Sarah pulled away from Michael. After walking a few steps, she turned to face him once again. With fists propped defiantly against her hips she announced her decision. "Then I'm going, too!"

He stared at her with his mouth agape. "Not a chance, Sarah!" he said, once he had regained control of his surprise. "There is no way in the world I would let you do that. We're not talking about a pleasant walk in the woods. O.K., you want me to admit to you that it's dangerous. Well, it is; and that is exactly why I can't allow you to come along. How much chance for success would I have if my mind was on your safety rather than on the situation I was walking into?"

Big Thomas walked over to Sarah just as she was preparing to object again. "You're not going to change his mind, you know. But, if it will make you feel better, I'm going along. I'll watch over him, and make sure he comes back in one piece." Thomas then turned to Everett and Michael. "Now, I'm sure I don't have to explain to you two why I would be a help to your adventure. Nobody knows rough terrain the way I do. Besides, when we get there maybe I will be able to find some heads to bash in. I haven't had a good tussle in a long time."

It did not take much convincing for them to see the wisdom of taking Thomas along. However, Michael would not change his mind as far as Sarah was concerned. She was to stay behind with Oliver as her protector.

That night around the campfire, the conversation was as subdued as the mood. Sarah's silence was due in part to her anger with Michael for his refusal to allow her to join the quest. She was also trying to formulate a plan that would force them to take her on the journey.

All talk of the coming journey had finally ceased. The darkening of the night sky was complete now, and their thoughts were turning to sleep. Everett's attention was elsewhere, however. His head was cocked to the side in deep concentration.

"Something is wrong," he said, quietly.

"What?" mumbled Oliver, as he was roused from near sleep. "What did you say?"

"Something is wrong out there," replied Everett as he stood staring into the enveloping darkness.

"I see what you mean, Everett," replied Thomas, as he got to his feet.

"What are you talking about?" inquired Sarah. "I don't hear anything, it's as quiet as could be out there."

"That's just what I mean," replied Thomas. "There's always night sounds in the woods, but now there are no sounds at all."

Everyone in the group stood as they grasped Thomas's remark. There should be noise of some sort. No one except Thomas was sure what form those night noises should take, but they all were aware now that the night was unnaturally still.

"So what is it?" whispered Sarah. She was surprised to hear herself being controlled by the situation so much that she was brought to a whisper.

Before anyone could offer an explanation, they were hit with the stench. The overpowering smell of rot rode through their camp, carried by the night breeze.

"Oh, my God," cried Sarah, as she recoiled in disgust. There was no escaping the putrid odor seeping through the camp. She did what she could by covering her nose and mouth with her hand as she knelt to the ground.

That was the only response anyone had a chance to make before the quiet was shattered by the sudden onslaught of charging wild animals.

So sudden was the charge, the two magicians, student and master alike, were taken completely by surprise. The once peaceful camp was stormed by fleeing animals. As though escaping from a raging forest fire, all manner of beasts fled side-by-side from the unseen danger. Normally natural enemies, wolves, bears, deer, boar, even small ground squirrels, charged down upon the startled group.

As Everett raised his hands to form the magical spell that would protect his friends, he was struck a glancing blow from a small deer that was wildly racing through the middle of the camp. Michael gave a shout born of terror as he saw a crazed boar, muzzle flecked with foam, head thrashing from side to side, aiming his flight straight toward Sarah.

Time stood still as he stared at the deadly tusks aimed at the woman he loved. Without thought, with a flourish of his hands, he froze the boar to the spot, a mere five feet from her. Before anyone had a chance to react further, Michael spread his arms wide. Following the sweep of his hands, a shimmering green light unfurled to envelop all of the members of the group.

As the heaviest concentration of animals reached the perimeter of the camp, the wondrous green light expanded to encompass the whole area in a dome of protection. All of the beasts flowed around the protective shield without a single misstep.

It was nearly five minutes later when the last animal had passed the area. "My God!" exclaimed Thomas. "What the hell is going on here? Something scared the hell out of those animals to cause that kind of stampede."

"The stench, Michael," groaned Everett from the ground where he still lay. "It's getting stronger. The shield you have erected won't keep that out. I'm afraid it also won't keep the cause of it out."

"What do you mean?" inquired Michael.

"I mean that wild charge was not natural. Oh, no doubt, natural fears were induced to cause such madness. But, I believe it was magic that did the inducing!"

As the five members of the camp began to look around with trepidation, the protective green light began to waver. Once again the night became startlingly hushed.

At first just a quiet chuckle could be heard breaking the silence. Then a loud malicious laugh rang through the darkness. "Fools!" called a voice from the night. "Your few precious moments of safety are over now.

"Brother," called the voice in the dark. "You have something I want, brother. Give it to me and I may at least spare that bitch you care so much about."

"Acantha!" called Michael. "The ruby, it's the ruby that causes you to do this. Fight against the evil of the stone!"

Again the wild, malignant laughing began beyond the perimeter of the camp.

"Oh, what a fool you truly are, Michael. I do what I wish. It is I that control the power, it does not control me."

"No, Acantha. I know you believe this to be true, but it is the ruby, it controls you."

"Enough of this!" screamed the voice of Acantha, as the specter of Croom lurched into the light of the campfire. Acantha's voice was coming from the corpse.

It was a chilling sight to see the long-dead man stalk into the camp. The smell of decayed flesh assaulted them with renewed vengeance as they stared at his broken visage. The new clothing he had stolen from the luckless Pitt's leather shop now hung on him like rags, torn and tattered. The blow that Pitts had delivered to his skull, caused a gaping hole above his left eye. The entire side of his face was beginning to droop at an alarming rate.

His steady shuffle into the camp came to a halt as he ran into the green shield erected by Michael. His look of confusion, as he turned from side to side to study the strange occurrence, did not match the scornful voice that spurted from him.

"It will take more than this paltry attempt at magic to keep me at bay, Michael."

With no outward sign of assistance from Croom, the green shield began to show small red cracks. They began to lengthen and spread, soon racing from side to side, then from top to bottom. In a matter of seconds the entire dome of green was covered with cracks, all glowing a violent red.

As the cracks began to pulsate, a sizzling hum could be heard running through the entire dome. There was a brilliant red flash and the dome disintegrated, the air sparkling with green and red motes floating to the ground.

Michael collapsed to his knees, exhausted from the demands of magic, as he realized his first test against Acantha had ended in failure. He did not have time to indulge in self-pity, however.

Immediately after the fall of the protective dome, Croom bulled his way straight toward Everett. The aged master raised his right hand; a ball of fire appeared from nowhere.

Everett hurled the fire-ball and scored a direct hit in the center of Croom's chest. Croom's hands flew up to protect his face an instant too late. Blisters appeared on the dead flesh of his face and his hair began to smolder. The leather clothing was charred and smoking.

Before Everett could unleash a second attack, a blinding red light exploded from Croom and streaked at Everett. The force of Acantha's magic lifted Everett from his feet and cast him to the far side of the camp. Everett had scarcely hit the ground before Thomas hurled himself at the intruder that had caused his friend such pain. Croom's strength was inhuman, but the giant mountain man threw his entire weight behind his charge. The pair crashed to the ground with the force of thunder. Thomas was up before they stopped rolling and hauled Croom up after him.

Oliver came rushing into the middle of the battle. He had snatched a burning limb from the fire, one end still aflame. With weapon lifted overhead, and in both hands, he charged at Croom. It was the first time he had seen this monster that had been pursuing Sarah. He was consumed with fear and anger as he rushed to Thomas's aid. His emotions gave voice to an anguished howl as he charged.

Feeling neither pain from Thomas' attack, nor fear of his two adversaries, Croom called upon his inhuman strength and heaved the giant into the charging Oliver. They fell together, in a tangle of arms and legs. Oliver was trapped beneath the stunned giant.

Michael was astounded with the speed of the pitched battle. It had been less than a minute since his protective dome had been destroyed. Now his friends lay in discarded heaps with Croom standing dispassionately in the center of the camp.

Croom turned to Michael and raised his right hand. "I warned you to give me the ring, Michael," said the voice of Acantha. "Now it is too late. I'll take it my way!"

Still on his knees, Michael again reacted instantly, throwing both hands in front of him toward Croom. A shaft of green light sprang from his hands; in the same instance a beam of red was racing to him from Croom. The two stood locked in battle, but not moving. The camp was bathed in the reflected light from the two beams. Splinters of red and green light splayed in all directions as the two forces of power met, centered between the two combatants.

Michael's shaft of light slowly began to dim and shrink, showing his power to be weaker than Acantha's. He fearfully glanced over to Sarah, still on the ground. She had crawled over to Oliver where he had landed on the ground after his attempt to help Thomas. She was watching Michael in his battle with Croom. Her expression showed her fear for Michael, as it was evident he was losing this test of strength as well.

Michael redoubled his efforts against Croom when he saw the concern reflected in Sarah's face. Her safety as well as the others' depended on his success, and there was no one available to give him aid now. Beginning slowly, then gaining in speed, Michael's shaft of light brightened and spread. Acantha's magic, being channeled through Croom, was now losing strength against Michael's superior power fed by the force of his will.

With an almost audible snap, the clearing was flooded with the brilliant emerald green light. The red glow from Croom's hand was extinguished. Croom looked at his empty hand in confusion as Michael wrapped him in the green light. His dread and anger had finally mastered his fear. He magically raised Croom from the ground and hurled him into the nearest tree. With broken bones showing through his skin and clothing, Croom still managed to regain his feet. Michael did not pause. Once again he lifted Croom on the end of the spear of light and hurled him into another tree. Before he could regain his feet Croom was streaking to a third tree, then a fourth.

"No!" came Acantha's strangled cry. "This battle has only begun Michael!" And with a shattering explosion that knocked Michael from his feet, Croom disappeared. Acantha had pulled her defeated assassin from the fray before he could be lost entirely.

As suddenly as it had started, the violence ended. Michael scanned the campsite to check on the condition of his friends. There were more than enough bruises and cuts to go around, but considering their ordeal, everyone seemed to have survived in relatively good condition. Glazed and shocked eyes stared back at him. Thomas was the only one not affected by the violence. With a large grin on his face, he sat next to Oliver.

"You seem amused, Thomas. What's so funny?" demanded Michael.

Thomas' grin widened as he pointed behind Michael. Still frozen in place was the boar that had stampeded straight for Sarah. Thomas looked around at the other members of the camp. "Dinner, anyone?"

CHAPTER 10

Acantha had watched the entire battle from the safety of her laboratory in the highest part of her keep. What she saw did not please her at all. Accepting the outcome of the battle with good graces was not her nature. She reacted to the outcome of the battle with her typical intolerance. She broke every piece of glass, most of the furniture, and the arm of one of her slaves in her anger.

She threw herself into the nearest unbroken chair to analyze what had gone wrong. She had been doing so well in the beginning. She had smashed through Michael's shield with ease, and had been able to defeat Everett and those other two clumsy fools with no problem. So what went wrong? She should have been able to overcome Michael's meager powers with very little effort.

Maybe it was the distance. After all, she was over one-hundred miles away. That must have been it, she decided; the distance. Michael was learning to call on the power of the emerald, and he was within feet of Croom during the fight, whereas she was so far away.

"No matter, you little fool," said Acantha with a sneer. "You told Everett you were coming South with him, and I'll be waiting."

With the grimace of bloodlust on her face, she rose and stormed to the door of her laboratory. Flinging the door open, she quickly twisted her head first to the left, then to the right, peering down the ornate hall.

At the end of the hallway, a startled slave stood frozen, mop and pail in hand.

"You! Get in here!" she bellowed, as she stood glaring with finger pointed wickedly at the man.

The poor fool shrieked and threw bucket and mop in the air. He turned and bolted for the stairwell at the end of the hall.

With a wave of her hand, Acantha stopped the fleeing slave in mid-stride. She flicked her wrist, and he began moving toward

Acantha. He did not move under his own volition, but rather as if he were tied to the end of a long rope, being pulled unwillingly to an evil end. He was pulled the entire length of the hall, screaming and kicking. Nearly insane with fear, the slave collapsed to the floor where he continued his fruitless attempts to escape Acantha's call.

He tried to slow his progress by clawing at the floor. Unfortunately the floor was stone and marble. His fingernails cracked, then tore. In the end he was dragged the length of the hall, coming to a stop at Acantha's feet.

"Your fingers are bleeding, fool," said Acantha with a smirk. "I don't know how much you have to spare, but I plan on taking some of it myself." She laughed as the poor man clamored to his feet in yet another attempt to escape.

"Come along now, I have no more time for your whimpering." She turned on her heel and strode toward her work bench. The slave was pulled from his feet by the invisible bonds that still held him. He tumbled and rolled behind her with every step she took. Upon reaching her worktable, she reached for the only unbroken piece of glassware in the room. She pulled the magical crystal bowl to her and looked down at the cringing slave. With a touch of her finger, he rose to a rigid standing position. She pulled his arm over to the table until his wrist hung like an unmoving branch above the crystal bowl.

"I don't know why you people persist in trying to deny me." She spoke as if to herself, unmindful of the terrified rolling eyes of her servant. She gazed at the veins in the man's wrist as she prepared to fill her need. Her thumb probed his wrist until she found the vein she wanted. With agonizing slowness she pressed the nail of her thumb into his wrist. The vein puffed, then began to swell, until it finally burst, filling the magical crystal bowl once again.

When the bowl was nearly full, she released her hold on the slave. His face was drawn and slack, gray bags sagging beneath dull eyes. He collapsed to the floor, passing out from his weakness. With a final wave of her wrist, the slave disappeared. He would awaken much later in the basement slave's quarters.

Once again waving her hand over the bowl, the fluid came to life, showing her the scene at Everett's camp. She would watch them. Soon enough he would make a mistake. When he did, she would be waiting to take advantage of it.

*     *     *     *     *

Michael and Sarah both sat near the campfire. The shock of the battle was finally beginning to wear off. The closeness to the light of the fire helped to push away their fears.

"Well, I think all this calls for some change in plans," said Michael, breaking the silence.

"What change do you mean?" asked Everett, suddenly alert to the possibility that Michael had changed his mind about the quest.

"I don't believe Sarah would be safe if we left her behind. Acantha has become vindictive enough that she would come after Sarah, even if it didn't help her to defeat us. She would be safest if she came along with us."

Everett sighed. "I suppose you're right."

"Well, don't sound so thrilled, Everett," Sarah replied petulantly. "I'll try not to get in the way, or slow you down."

"No, I'm not concerned about you slowing us down, I'm concerned about your safety. Whether you go with us or stay behind, I'm afraid you're at risk."

Sarah was immediately sorry for snapping at Everett. He had been a good friend of Michael's and deserved better treatment than that. "I'm sorry, Everett. I know you're concerned. I'm just jumpy because of all that's happened."

Oliver leaned closer to the fire. "Well, I guess I know what I'll be doing for the next couple of months. And not a word from you, Sarah, you're not going without me."

Thomas stopped Sarah's imminent objection by joining the conversation. "So, we're all going together, that's all settled. What I would like to know is how you managed to beat that creature. You said your magic isn't strong enough to control that stone of yours, but it looked to me as if you did a pretty good job."

"What do you think, Everett?" asked Michael. "I was controlling the stone. It wasn't acting on its own this time. I don't even know if I could do it again."

Everett leaned back against the log he was resting on. "Well, maybe you listened more during your classes than either you or I realized. I think much of magic is controlled through desire and strength of will. The stronger your will to battle this evil, the more power you are able to call upon. When you saw that we -- especially Sarah -- were lost without you, your will power was at its strongest. Just speculation at this point, of course, but at least it's an educated guess."

Michael rose from his place near the fire and walked to the edge of the clearing. He stared into the night for a couple of minutes, deep in thought before returning to the campfire. He stood near the flames as he looked around at the friends that had all offered to accompany him. "If you are all going to go with us, you deserve to know what Everett said to me to convince me to undertake this quest."

The next hour was devoted to telling his friends about the history of the enchanted talismans, and his ancestors' place in history.

If Michael had thought his ancestors' deeds would change his friends' opinion of him, he had misjudged them. At the end of the story, all were still committed to the journey. If anything, their resolve was strengthened when they learned of the danger that would be loose in the world if Acantha was successful in her attempt to control both rings.

*     *     *     *     *

Acantha had watched the entire conversation at the campsite. She continued to watch, even after all of Michael's followers had retired for the night. They had set a schedule where each of them would take turns staying up and watch over the camp that would extend until daybreak. All of the members of the camp were to take a turn, even Sarah. A plan began to grow as Acantha watched the camp. Soon she saw her chance. The second camp guard of the night had wandered too far from the protection of the group. She could have her way with this one without any interference.

The call of nature must be answered, even for those on a majestic quest. So it was that one of Michael's followers was caught in a most compromising position. From the fog that was beginning to settle on the mountain top, a figure was beginning to appear. A portion of the fog separated and began to coalesce until the figure of Acantha stood before the defenseless guard. The figure was only a trick, a likeness of the sorceress, but when it pointed a finger at the guard, movement was impossible.

"My, it seems I've caught you with your pants down, doesn't it?" Acantha leaned her head back in laughter to enjoy to the fullest her prisoner's humiliation. The laughter, as was the voice, was light, however. It had the feathery softness of the fog itself.

The camp guard was struck with a piercing terror. Muscles were locked rigid. Previously warm, dry skin became cold and soaked with frigid perspiration. Stark, unblinking eyes stared into the night. It was obvious evil magic was making an appearance.

The guard was struck with a piercing terror. His muscles were locked rigid. Previously warm, dry skin became cold and soaked with frigid perspiration. Stark, unblinking eyes stared into the night. The guard knew evil magic was making an appearance.

"I have filled you with fear, have I not?" inquired the specter.

No answer was forthcoming, none was expected.

"I have a special curse for you. You will work to my ends. Do you understand what I am saying to you?"

The helpless victim's head bobbed up and down in answer. It was impossible to control the motion.

"I will come to you from time to time and give you instructions. You will carry out my instructions, exactly as I give them. Do you understand what I am telling you?"

Once again the victim's head bounced up and down in the affirmative.

"After you have done what I tell you, you will forget that I have spoken to you, and the act that I willed you to do.

"Go now, return to your feeble attempt at standing guard. When I need you again, I will seek you out. You may return to what you were doing now." Once again the soft peel of laughter as the fog broke apart and swirled into the night.

With a snap, the spell was cancelled. Acantha's unwilling accomplice fell to the ground as the restricted muscles were set free. Now unaware of the last few minutes of entrapment, the camp guard silently cursed the hidden root that must have caused the fall. Nearing the time of the guard change, Acantha's accomplice returned to camp to awaken the next person to take their turn. That being done, it was to bed and a peaceful night's sleep.

Inside her laboratory, Acantha's mood had improved greatly. She fairly danced across the room to the same chair she had occupied earlier in the evening. This time she sat with a smug smile on her beautiful face. She leaned the chair back on two legs and propped her feet on a shattered table in front of her. The future promised to be very amusing.

## CHAPTER 11

Sitting on a hill just south of Monterey, Sarah looked down at the village that used to be her home. It had been a hard, week-long journey from the mountains above Cruz Town to the hills of Monterey.

"It's beautiful from up here, isn't it?"

"Yes," replied Michael. "This was the first view I had of Monterey when I got here. It was early morning then, everything was so fresh and clean looking. I fell in love with the beauty here the very first time I saw it."

The scene they looked over was majestic. The hillside they sat on was covered with eucalyptus, pine, and cypress trees, and numerous flowering bushes. The woodlands continued down the hillside in an explosion of greenery. They obscured the remaining derelict buildings of a past age. The onslaught of the wild growth ceased only when met by the superior strength of the ocean.

To the north, the pair could trace the arc of the bay by looking at the miles-long strand of beach that curved like the sliver of the moon. On a very clear day, they would be able to see Cruztown as a hazy point, now nearly lost to the distance.

Michael brought their break to an end. "Well, I guess we should get back to the others. We have quite a few plans to make."

"Before we go back, I have a question," said Sarah. "It's been bothering me that I have been gone so long without telling Charlie what happened. He's probably worried to death."

"You're probably right. What do you want to do?"

"I want to send him a message telling him I'm okay."

"I don't know if that would be wise," said Michael.

"Why? Do you really believe Acantha doesn't know where we are, or that we're heading south? Besides, I won't tell him where we are, or that we are going to Acantha's keep. I just want him to know that we are all right. Thomas is going into town for supplies. He could contact Charlie for me."

"Okay, we'll tell Everett what you want to do, and if he says it would be all right, then I don't see why not."

"Oh, thank you, Michael," said Sarah, as she jumped into his arms.

When they finally returned to camp, they found Everett deep in trance, while Thomas was inspecting his bow, with Oliver overseeing the inspection.

"So, Thomas. Do you have everything in mind that we'll need for our trip?" inquired Michael.

"Yeah, in fact it looks like I'll have to add a new bow to my list. I just found a hairline crack in this one. It could give out on me any time. I don't have time to make a new one myself."

"Are you sure you want to go to Monterey by yourself?" asked Sarah. "I mean, considering all the supplies you have to carry when you return."

"No problem, Sarah. I'm used to working hard. It keeps me strong, you know."

"I don't think you need to worry about suddenly going weak, Thomas," said Oliver. "You're the strongest man I've ever seen, and I've been around working men all my life."

"Well, the truth is, I like a little solitude once in a while. That's why I chose to live by myself in the mountains in the first place."

"Okay," replied Oliver. "At least let me help you on the hunt. The better we do with that, the more credits you will have to spend."

If they were lucky, all of the supplies would be paid for with fresh meat. Thomas and Oliver would bring down a good-sized deer. The deer would be taken to one of the taverns in town where they would receive credit. The credits would then be bartered for the needed supplies.

In order to take full advantage of the remaining daylight, Thomas and Oliver decided to leave as soon as possible. Thomas took the lead and made for the animal trail he had spotted earlier in the day. He bent down to show Oliver the deer tracks hidden beneath disturbed leaves.

"There's a stream down there at the end of this trail," said Thomas softly. "We'll find a good place near the stream and set up watch."

The pair continued on for another couple of hundred yards until the stream was in view. At that point Thomas silently pointed at a tree just off the path.

Oliver merely nodded ascent. Having hunted with Thomas often in the last two weeks, he knew what was expected.

After an hour of sitting ten feet off the ground, on another limb close to Thomas in the tree, Oliver spotted a deer approaching the stream.

He nudged Thomas to draw his attention to the animal. Thomas had already seen the deer and dismissed it. He shook his head to negate Oliver's suggestion.

"Female," whispered Thomas.

"Very tender, for a big man," replied Oliver, just as hushed.

"Nothing tender about it, she has young following her."

It wasn't much longer before their waiting paid off. A large stag was carefully picking its way along the trail.

Thomas had but one arrow left, so he waited patiently for the animal to reach the nearest point to them. He silently notched the arrow and slowly pulled the string taut. He sat motionless, with drawstring nearly touching his cheek, until the stag was right where he wanted it.

With the vibration of the string in his ears, he loosed the arrow. Over the hum of the string, he heard the crack of the bow as if broke after sending its last arrow. But the arrow was true, it struck the stag just above and behind the front leg, piercing the heart. The deer was dead on the ground before the pair could quit their places in the tree. Once down, they ran to the fallen animal where Thomas did the blood-letting. They returned to the camp, with their prize slung over Thomas' shoulders, just as darkness was falling.

"Okay, we've got payment for our supplies," stated Thomas, as he deposited the deer. "It cost me my bow, but this fellow should prove to be enough to get everything we need plus a new bow for me."

"You both did well, Thomas," said Everett. He seemed quite restful after his time in meditation. "Do you leave in the morning then?"

"At first light. Too late now. I'd break my leg in the dark if I tried to go tonight."

"Tomorrow will be soon enough."

"It's time for rest now," said Sarah, as she approached the men. "I've got dinner ready."

"Ah....bless you, Sarah," replied Thomas. "I haven't eaten in hours!"

The next morning, shortly after dawn, the inhabitants of Monterey witnessed a huge man, with a matchingly large stag over his shoulders, walk into town.

He had stopped only long enough to ask directions to the taverns of the town. He needed to trade his stag in for credits, and wanted to know where he could get the best deal. The mountain man had received directions to the two best taverns in town. Thomas already knew where he wished to go, but did not want the townsmen to suspect he was anything other than an itinerant hunter that did not know the village.

He eventually reached the front of Sarah's tavern. Waiting for her return, Charlie had kept the place open and in good repair. He was in fact already at work, even this early in the day. The man Thomas had been sent to see was busily sweeping the entrance when he approached. "Good morning, sir," offered Thomas. "I was told by your friends here in the village that this is the best tavern in town, with the best meals."

Charlie turned to stare open-mouthed at the towering man confronting him. He continued to stare at Thomas as though mesmerized.

"Well, as you can see," Thomas continued, "I've had good fortune in the hunt. It's much more than I would ever be able to eat myself -- at least in one sitting," he said with a chuckle. "I wonder if you would be needing fresh meat to serve to your patrons?"

"Uh...well, maybe so," Charlie finally managed to say. "At least, that is, uh...I guess."

Charlie looked around the street as if in hopes of finding someone to help him deal with this strange man.

"I mean, the young lady that owns the tavern here has up and disappeared, and well, I'm running the place for her 'til she gets back."

"You seem real sure she's coming back. You're not worried about her?"

"Well, not really. You see, her good friend Oliver has up and disappeared, too. And Michael...that's her man. So, I figure Oliver has taken them on a trip across the bay, or something."

Charlie paused to scratch his head. "The thing is though, she's never been out of the village before. And I don't see that Oliver would take them across the bay without telling me, don't you see? Or at least telling someone."

"Well," replied Thomas, "I have some good news for you that will set your mind at ease. But perhaps first we could do something with this stag. It's becoming a mite bit heavy."

Charlie immediately dropped his broom, and reached for the deer to help Thomas unload his burden. Thomas shook his head at the offer of help, and requested to be shown to the back room.

"Oh, yeah, sure. Just follow me."

Once in the kitchen area of the tavern, Thomas unloaded his burden.

"Now, before I begin working on this for you, I have some important news." He reached inside his leather jerkin and pulled out a hand-written message addressed to Charlie. "This is from Sarah."

Charlie grabbed the message from Thomas, and with shaking hands began to read. The note did not explain the trouble they were in, but did let him know that she was all right and with her friends.

"I don't understand. Why didn't she let me know that she was going? It says here she'll be gone for a long time yet. Where's she going?"

"She didn't let you know before hand, Charlie, because she didn't know herself. She's going south, that's all I can tell you about her plans; except of course that she is with friends. She hopes that will be enough for you."

"Yeah, well...if that's what she wants."

Thomas saw the crestfallen look on the simple man's face and felt sympathy. He explained that Sarah cared a great deal for him, or she would not have gone to such trouble to get word to him.

"She's depending on you, Charlie."

"She is?" replied Charlie, with an awed expression.

"Sure, she needs someone to keep the tavern open and running for her while she is gone."

"That's me!" said Charlie with chest puffing.

"And not a word to anyone until I'm out of town, Charlie, I don't want a bunch of questions to answer. After I'm gone you can tell anyone you want that you have heard from Sarah."

"You've got it, partner!" Charlie stuck his hand out to Thomas to shake on keeping his end of the bargain.

It was nearly three hours later when Thomas left Sarah's tavern. The butchering had been done, and his pocket was full of credits that would be needed to purchase the group's supplies. Charlie knew that Thomas would be back for dinner before returning to his campsite, and agreed to keep quiet until the next day when the group would be on its way. Thomas spent the rest of the afternoon bargaining for the supplies that would be needed. The final purchase that he made was for the replacement of his ruined bow.

He was fully laden when he returned to see Charlie.

"Hey, Thomas. How come you're always carryin' something when I see you?" Charlie felt as though he was speaking with an old cherished friend since he found Thomas to be a friend of Sarah's.

"Just my lot in life, Charlie. What's for dinner?"

"Venison stew, of course. Are you ready for some?"

"Bring it on."

Thomas piled his supplies next to his chosen table, and sat down to await his meal. It was nearing the time when the fishermen would be coming in for their own dinner, so the tavern was slowly beginning to fill. He was finishing his stew when three seamen from a visiting supply vessel entered. These were rough men use to the hard life, both in work and play. One of the men led the other two to the last empty table. He was a large man with unruly red hair and a flushed face. His friends followed behind like puppies, wanting to please their master.

"Hey, squid-breath," hollered the leader. "You had better have something for us to eat today besides that shit you've been calling fish stew." His cronies howled with laughter as they watched Charlie flinch from his words.

"You tell him, Red. We're going to make fish stew outta him if he doesn't have something good to eat."

Charlie left the main room, and when he returned he was carrying a tray with three bowls of the venison stew.

"No fish tonight. I've got fresh venison for you," he stated, as he sat the bowls in front of the derisive men.

Charlie was turning to leave the table when the seaman called Red grabbed him by the back of the shirt. "Where do you think you're going, you stinking chunk of fish-bait?"

The man stood as he pulled Charlie back to the table. He was much larger than Charlie and easily overpowered him.

Grabbing him by the back of the neck, he pushed Charlie's face nearly into the table. "Do you see any beer on this table, mister?"

It was all Charlie could do to shake his head no.

"Then get over there and bring us some." With his last state-ment he pushed Charlie across the room with sufficient force to make him stumble into the bar. All three of the men were laughing so hard they did not see the large man charging at them.

Thomas did not even slow as he hit the table. With a thunder-ous crash, he knocked over table, chairs, and men. He was hauling one of Red's mates to his feet even before they realized they had been attacked. The first man to feel Thomas' wrath was the lucky one. Thomas, with one hand clasped on the man's shirt collar, and the other grabbing the seaman's trousers by the seat, was rushing to the door dragging the man with him.

One of the local fishermen, quick to see the developing fight, jumped to open the door for Thomas. Thomas' victim found himself flying through the door, then crashing to the dirty road outside. With the breath knocked from him, it was all the seaman could do to sit up and be thankful he was no longer in the bar with the enraged giant.

Red and his remaining cohort looked up at Thomas as he stalked back to the center of the room. Red was glaring at Thomas, ready for the brawl. His buddy was staring wistfully at the door, wishing it was he that had just gone through it. Escape for him would not come so quickly, however. The door was blocked by the locals. They were not brave enough to help Charlie, but now that a rescuer had been found, they were going to make certain that the abusive bullies did not leave until Thomas was done with them.

Red sized up his opponent as a bigger and stronger man, but lacking the ruthlessness that was necessary in a tavern brawl. As he came to his feet, Red grabbed a nearby fallen glass mug from the floor. Never taking his eyes from Thomas, he broke the glass on the overturned table. He charged at the giant with the shards of glass extended before him.

Thomas pulled a vacated chair from beside him and flung it at the charging man's feet. Red tripped on the low-flying chair and somersaulted through the air, the glass falling from his hand. When he hit the floor, Thomas quickly yanked him to his feet, his fist smashing into Red's face in almost the same instant. Red stumbled and fell against the bar.

With blood erupting from his broken nose, Red began to reevaluate his opponent. He began to believe this man might well be ruthless enough to win the fight. He looked to his friend, still sitting on the floor. "What the hell you doing on the floor, you stupid bastard! Get your ass up here and help me!"

Red's friend began to furtively seek any route of escape. Another door, a window, anything that would get him out of the tavern, rather than face this avenging force.

Thomas looked at the men blocking the door. "If this guy wants to leave, let him. It's this red-headed fella I want to play with."

At Thomas' words, Red's man jumped to his feet and flew to the door.

"Go to hell, you shit! I'll take care of this stupid bear myself!" shouted Red at the man's retreating back. His face twisted in pure hatred, he raised his fists to protect his battered face and stalked toward Thomas.

Thomas had been in more than a few brawls over the years and knew what to expect. Red's first punch was a strong but wild looping right roundhouse, aimed at Thomas' face. Thomas easily blocked the expected punch with his left arm, and drove a right straight into Red's already broken nose. The man fell to the floor with an anguished howl, clutching his battered face.

He rolled over onto his knees, and struggled to his feet. Staggering over to one of the tables, he clawed at a sharpened knife that had been placed there for someone's forgotten dinner. Grabbing the knife, he faced Thomas again. Crouched low, he began to move forward.

A vicious smile split Red's face as he began to lunge at Thomas. Before he could complete his charge a full, corked beer bottle whistled through the air, catching Red just above the temple. He crashed to the floor, unconscious even before he fell.

Next to the bar, where the bottle began its flight, stood Charlie. "Well, he said he wanted a beer. So...I gave him one!"

The bar erupted in laughter and cheering as the local fishermen surrounded Thomas and Charlie, patting backs and giving congratulations. Some of the men carried the unconscious seaman back to his ship. They stayed to speak to the captain, to insure that Red would not return to shore as long as the ship was in port. The rest of the men stayed to help Thomas and Charlie clean up the mess from the fight.

It was well past midnight when Thomas finally left Sarah's tavern. He was greatly pleased with the day. He had secured all the supplies they would need for the journey south, made some new friends, and even had a chance to crack a couple of heads.

With his backpack fully loaded, and both hands occupied with two more full packs, Thomas left Monterey humming to himself. There was a swagger to his step.

CHAPTER 12

Michael's group followed the trail up the hill from Monterey. This was one of the old concrete ways, from the days before the Magicians' War. Most of the concrete was gone now, but they had no trouble following the cleared area where it had once been.

The wonderful weather they had been having finally deserted them. The ever-present fog, that clung to the peninsula during the very early and very late hours, would normally burn off when the sun gained strength in the late morning. Today, however, even though it was past noon, the fog was so thick they could not see more than fifty yards ahead of them. With the fog came a slow but steady rain.

"Good heavens," complained Everett. "How do you people ever get use to this fog? The dampness goes right through to the bone."

"I can't say I like the rain, Everett," replied Sarah, "but I love the fog. Don't you find it beautiful, the way it rolls through the tree tops?"

"As far as I'm concerned, it could roll right on out of here." Everett looked over at Michael. "So, how do you feel, Michael?"

"What? I feel fine, why?"

"Well, I've been thinking about what will happen when we reach Acantha's keep. Your magic is going to have to be much stronger than it is now, if we are to succeed. And if you are up to it, I think now is a good time to begin to strengthen your powers."

Michael was quiet for a minute while they walked. He was drenched from the steady fall of the light rain. Water was dripping from the hair that was plastered to his forehead. His clothes were drenched and clinging to his body.

"I guess I'm up to it, Everett. I just don't know what I should do to make my powers stronger. I've had years of schooling, with you as instructor, I don't see how I'm going to advance so much further in such a short time."

"You have the emerald now," replied Everett. "You must learn how to tap the well of power it represents.

"I was just thinking, here we are slopping through soaking wet grass and weeds, rain drenching our clothes, making them stick to us -- and you could do something about it!"

"Me?" Michael stopped walking and looked over to Everett.

Thomas and Oliver, having taken the lead, also stopped and turned back to watch the two magicians.

"How in the world am I supposed to make it stop raining? I don't have that kind of power, even with the emerald."

"You don't know yet what kind of power you have," responded Everett. "Anyway, I wasn't talking about stopping the rain. I was just talking about us getting wet."

Michael paused to look up at the falling rain. "I don't know, Everett. I don't even know how I was able to call on the emerald the last time. But here goes nothing."

Michael closed his eyes to concentrate and went into a light trance. He slowly raised one hand over his head, passing it from front to back in a sweeping motion.

The rain falling on them began to slow, finally coming to a stop. Oliver looked around in a circle. It was clear that it was still raining, it was falling on all sides of them; but not where they stood.

"Damn! I think I'm beginning to like this magic stuff," said Oliver. "How the hell did you do that?"

Michael opened his eyes, and grinned at the old fisherman. "I couldn't stop the rain, so I moved it. It's just flowing around us, that's all."

"Yes sir, real convenient," said Thomas.

They walked for nearly an hour before they noticed that it had stopped raining altogether. They were on the far side of the hill from Monterey. To their right the shoreline was nearly a mile distant, having reached the distant point of the peninsula. It would once again curve toward them until they were walking near the beaches. This would happen in about two more hours. Shortly before they reached the end of their day's journey, they spotted a solitary man walking the path toward them.

As he neared them, they could see he was a tall, slender man with stooped posture. He was swathed in a heavy coarse brown robe. Although his robe was the same color as Everett's, this man wore his as though he was imprisoned by it. His hands were clasped in front of him, but lost in the voluminous folds of the sleeves. His head, and most of his face, was hidden by the hood that draped across the front.

Michael's group stopped as the man approached them. He seemed to have just now noticed them. He peered at them from the shadows of his hood with jaundiced eyes.

"I am Ezekiel," he stated. He stared at Everett, being the elder of the group, waiting for response.

"Well met, Ezekiel," said Everett. He continued by introducing his traveling companions, avoiding mention of where they were heading, or for what purpose.

"You have the look about you of weary travelers. May my brothers and I offer you sanctuary?"

"You speak as a holy man," replied Everett, without offering an answer to the question.

"Indeed, this is true," replied Ezekiel, as he bowed his head. "I am a brother of The Church of the Second Millennium."

Michael and Everett shared a wordless glance at each other.

"I trust this does not cause you consternation," Ezekiel added, as he watched the two men.

"Of course not, brother. It's just that it has been long since we have met one with your convictions."

The shrouded figure sighed as though with great burden. "No doubt. Our numbers have diminished over the years. There are not many that can uphold the strict tenets of our faith. But, regarding my offer of sanctuary from the night," Ezekiel's eyes pierced them with

suspicion. "Would it not be preferable to spending the night blan-
keted by the cold, damp fog?"

As Michael moved to decline the offer, Everett reached out to
take his arm. Michael held his peace.

"It would be quite preferable, and we thank you," the old man
said for the group.

As Ezekiel turned to lead them along the path south, Michael
asked Everett what had possessed him to accept the offer. Everett
explained to Michael that it was better to have danger in view, rather
than waiting around the corner to surprise you.

Sarah moved closer to them. "I'm missing something here,
aren't I? Who is this man, and what is this church he is from?"

"The Church of the Second Millennium, and keep your voice
down," responded Everett. "They are a very rigid cult. They believe
that magicians are demons of the devil."

"What?" exclaimed Sarah.

"Shhhh. Please, keep your voice down."

"Why are we going with him if his church hates magicians?"

"Because if we didn't, they would rightly suspect that we had
something to hide. Pass the word to Oliver and Thomas, say nothing
about who we are or why we are heading south."

As they continued along the route south, a large building
became visible ahead and to the left. It looked to be twice as old as
any of the ramshackled buildings Sarah was familiar with from the
village. It also seemed to have withstood the test of time much better.

The building was set back quite a way from the roadway the
group was upon, however the details of the building were easily seen.
It was a heavy, oppressive building, constructed of brick and mortar,
and ancient dark wood.

As they turned from the path and began to make their way up
to the church, Ezekiel spoke for the first time since their meeting.

"You will have noticed, I surmise, that our church is in remark-
ably good repair. Since its construction this building has been tended

to. Never has it been empty, and never has it housed other than the children of God."

As they approached the building, they first came upon a wall surrounding it. The wall was made of the same stone and mortar. The massive front gate was closed.

Ezekiel reached for a cord that was suspended from the wall. Inside, the muffled peal of a bell could be heard. They stood in silence waiting for the summons to be answered.

From behind the gate, the travelers could hear the sliding of the bolt, releasing the lock from the gate.

When the door opened, they could see two brothers of the church waiting to greet their visitors. Neither of the two looked as ominous as Ezekiel.

"Please, come in," said one of the brothers. His face was fixed with an easy smile. "Do you seek refuge from the night?"

"If it would not be too inconvenient," replied Everett. "We will be resuming our journey at first light."

"No inconvenience at all," replied the brother who had just spoken. "We welcome travelers."

Once inside the gate introductions were made. The church brother they had spoken with was named Jerimias. Wrapped in the same coarse, burdensome robe, he was nevertheless much more congenial than the morose Ezekiel.

Jerimias led them to the rooms they would be using for the night. The large main hallway of the church was bare of amenities, and the ceiling was fully thirty feet over their heads. Their footsteps sounded sharply on the wooden floor and echoed through the hall.

Once across the hall, Ezekiel disappeared through a heavy wooden door. Michael and his friends followed Jerimias, and found a stairwell of stone steps leading down to the lower parts of the church. The walls were close, and gave the feeling that they were slowly moving inward, to trap the unholy. Escape from the stairwell came in the form of another hallway, this one being dark and moist. It was lit with large candles. The light, however, was dim as the candles were spaced more than thirty feet apart.

Jerimias turned to address his followers. "You may take the first five cells along the left side of the wall. They have been empty for many years and may smell musty, but they will provide you with safe and protected sleep.

"When you have unloaded your supplies, come back upstairs. Our evening meal and worship will commence within the hour."

When Jerimias left, everyone began to speak at once.

"What in the world are we doing here, Everett?" asked Michael.

"I don't think I like this place," declared Oliver.

"Gotta admit, I'd rather be under the open sky," said Thomas.

Sarah said, "Michael, these men are dangerous. I can feel it. Why are we here?"

"Everett, why in God's name did you agree to come here? You know what The Church of the Second Millennium believes," said Michael.

"Enough," snapped Everett. "We are here for good reasons. If we had declined the offer we would have been under suspicion. Further, we are not in danger as long as these men do not know we are magicians".

After speaking, Everett softened his tone. "The main reason that I accepted, however, is much more important. I want you all to understand the nature of the quest we have undertaken. We are going into the very lair of Acantha. Once there we are going to make an attempt to steal her mode of power right off her finger.

"This will take great courage on everyone's part. You are right, we are in danger as long as we are under this roof. If that prospect frightens you too much to function properly, if you cannot control your fears, then you do not belong on this venture. Call it a test if you will, but you must learn to handle your fears. You must be able to look into the face of fear, and still perform."

He paused here to smile at his friends. "Trust in Michael, trust in me. We will let no harm come to you here. Now, go to your rooms and unload your burdens. We will go upstairs shortly to join our hosts."

Michael was unloading his pack when Sarah entered his room. "Michael, just what is The Church of the Second Millennium, and what do they believe in? You seemed just as upset about being here as I am."

"I didn't mean to cause you concern," said Michael as he turned to her. "I was just surprised Everett would allow us to come here."

"But, why, Michael? What does this church represent that worries you?"

"Here, sit down, I'll try to explain the church to you."

With Sarah sitting next to him on the thin cot, Michael told her what he knew about the church.

"After the Magicians' War, a particularly zealous religious cult explained the war and resultant disappearance of so many people, as the War of Armageddon, and consequently the rapture....the rapture being when all true believers are taken to heaven.

"After the rapture, Satan is to be the lord of the earth for a millennium. The Church of the Second Millennium believes they are now living during the time of Satan's rule. The proof to that assertion is evidenced in the presence of magic in the world. Magicians are therefore tools of the devil. The brothers of the church feel it is their duty to find and dispose of the magicians of the world. To their way of thinking, they must eradicate all magic from the face of the earth," said Michael, completing his story.

"So, if they find out you and Everett are magicians, they will try to kill you." She looked into Michael's eyes. "I see what Everett meant when he says we must conquer our fear during this trip. I have not thought of losing you, until now."

She opened her arms, moving into Michael's embrace.

"Don't worry," whispered Michael. "We'll be careful."

Returning upstairs, they found Ezekiel waiting for them at the head of the stairs.

"Are you ready for our evening devotionals and then dinner?" he asked.

"Thank you. It would be an honor, Ezekiel," responded Michael.

Without a further word, Ezekiel turned and led them through the halls of the church. Upon reaching a large darkened room to the side of the main building, they found the entire membership of the church, nearly fifty men, gathered in silence. They were led to a bench near the end of the room. Ezekiel passed them five large squares of cloth, dark brown and coarse, like the robes. These they were directed to drape over their heads.

"You must be covered when communing with God," he explained.

The five visitors did as instructed, then turned their gaze to the front of the room. In the very front, there was a podium where six men were gathered. Two were to the left of center, and two were to the right. They were on their knees, heads bowed, and hands clasped in front.

In the center of the podium, a fifth man stood next to an ornate chair on a pedestal. The sixth man was sitting in the chair. The man had surpassed what would be considered old age many years ago; he was, in fact, ancient.

Even though covered by the heavy brown robe, the travelers could see he was frail beyond description. His robe hung about him like a funeral shroud. The hands that extended beyond the folds of the sleeves were skeletal. The face protruding from the hood was very nearly a skull.

The figure raised his arm from his lap, the hand hanging from the wrist, seemingly too heavy to be held straight. At the gesture, the church body dropped to their knees, almost in a single movement. After a brief hesitation, and a wordless glance at Everett for direction, the travelers did the same. The hooded brother standing next to the chair leaned down to put his ear next to the old man's mouth. When the brother stood again to speak, Michael and his friends recognized the voice belonging to Jeremias.

"Brothers. We, of the 144,000. We have been entrusted by God to spread his word among his people of the earth. Our duty has never been more difficult, our challenge has never been greater."

Once again Jeremias leaned down to the old man in the chair. "Our numbers have dwindled," he continued after he rose from hearing the old man's instructions. "To continue our service, our ranks must once again swell. We must spread our word and our purpose to all men."

He raised his hands over his head as he gave final instructions. "We must seek out the demons that are aligned with the Devil! They must perish before any more souls are lost!"

"They must perish!" chorused the church body. "They must perish!"

"Pray brothers! Pray that they may perish!"

The next fifteen minutes were spent in silent prayer. Michael, Sarah, Thomas, and Oliver exchanged concerned looks during this time. Everett was as still as a statue. Head bowed, appearing to be in prayer.

Once back in the cellars, safe among their rooms, Sarah met with Michael. "They give me the shivers, Michael," she said as she held her arms crossed close to her chest. "You could have heard a mouse scamper across the floor during the prayers. It was such an ominous silence."

"Well, I tried to impress on you that they are fanatics."

"The 144,000 that Jeremias mentioned, what did that mean?" she asked.

"I do know a bit about that. We studied them as our main danger. There is a holy book from the time before the Magicians' War. That is where this cult originated. They perverted the teachings of that great book to meet their own purposes. The 144,000 refers to a special group of people that are supposed to be sent by God to teach his word. They feel that the members of their church are that group. I don't know where they got the idea that they are supposed to go out and murder all the magicians they can find. But, that seems to be their goal in life."

"Well, promise me you won't be one of those magicians that they prey on, Michael," said Sarah as she moved into his arms, oblivious to her unintentional pun.

"I'll do my best," he said with a smile. "But, for now, you had better get back to your own room. I don't think they would be pleased to find you in mine. In fact, they would probably find that as sinful as being a magician."

"All right, I'll go. But, I'm not going to get any sleep in this place."

All of the travelers would have a difficult time finding sleep tonight. One of them would be visited by Acantha. It was time to call upon her ensorcelled accomplice.

CHAPTER 13

As the time neared midnight, one of Michael's friends left their cell. Acantha had made her visit. The hall outside of the small rooms housing the travelers was much darker now. Some of the candles had gone out, others were flickering weakly, having nearly burned out. The shadowy figure did not flow smoothly through the hallway; rather stumbled in spastic movements, as if not aware of what the body was doing. The stairs were reached and climbed by stiff unyielding legs, the eyes were glazed and staring.

Upon reaching the top of the stairs, the figure silently opened the door to the main hallway and waited, listening for sounds of movement. Hearing none, the person crossed the hallway, still in darkness, heading toward the large room where services were held earlier.

In the front of the room, near the altar, one of the hooded brothers was kneeling in prayer. The traveler backed into the shadows near the entrance, waiting for the holy man to begin to leave.

The brother was in prayer for nearly twenty minutes before rising. The intruder in the shadows had not moved a muscle the entire time. Now, as the figure in the coarse brown robes began to leave, the person hiding in the shadows spoke.

"Stop, brother," whispered the intruder. "Do not look behind you, my knife is very sharp, and I am quite willing to test it."

The church brother halted, as ordered. When he spoke there was no evidence of fear in his voice. "You threaten me with death. Do you not know that if you kill me, I will then be with my Father?"

"I have no wish to send you to your Father," replied the whispering voice. "I have a message that you must carry to your church leaders. There are magicians defiling your church. You gave them rest for the night, and sustenance, even now they are asleep beneath your feet. Tell your elders. There are magicians in The Church of the Second Millennium."

The brother started with the news, nearly turning to see the shadow hiding in the corner. He stopped when the figure hissed a warning.

"How do you know this? Are you one of them?"

"Never mind who I am, just do as you are told."

"How am I to know you are telling the truth?" asked the brother.

He was answered by silence. When he finally looked around, the corner was empty. Whoever he had spoken with had left. Wasting no time, the brother raced to the room of his elder.

Brother Jeremias' room was as austere as any of the brothers'. The one privilege that he allowed himself, due to his rank, was the location of his room. It was situated on the main floor, with a door leading out to a flower garden. When his breathless fellow church-man came rushing to his front door, he was standing in the flower garden, marveling at the brilliance of the midnight stars.

He quit the garden and reentered his room when he heard the fervent pounding on the door. Upon opening the door, the breathless brother paused to give a respectful bow before delivering his strange message.

"Please, Brother David, slow yourself. Come into my cell and make yourself clear."

"It's true I tell you!" continued the upset brother. "Whoever spoke, did so quietly enough that I had to strain to make out the words. I could not even make out whether it was a man or woman. But I am certain they said there is a magician in the church.

"Brother Jeremias, we must destroy the visitors!"

"Not so fast, brother. We must first be sure our course is the proper one. It is God's duty to decide who is righteous and who is not. I will give you a list of names. I want you to bring these brothers to my garden."

When David had left, Jeremias returned to his garden. The night was quiet and peaceful. He strolled through the garden with head bowed, hands clasped behind his back. He contemplated the news he had been brought, and worried over what his actions would be.

The travelers would need to be tested. There was no question about that. But how does one go about capturing -- how many, all five? – magicians to put them to the test. If they were indeed the Devil's agents, they could destroy the entire monastery, killing all of God's children.

Their teachings were clear. Faith, and trust in their God, would be sufficient to bind the powers of the magicians. He certainly hoped so. He had never been confronted with the possibility of magicians in the church before.

Soon the brothers that Jeremias had requested began to arrive at his cell. They were shown to the garden, as the cell was too small to hold five grown men.

Jeremias was joined by Brother Ezekiel, Brother David and three other elders. The other three were just beneath Jeremias' station.

Brother Ahira was a large man of stern countenance, vigilant in his duties. He had been with the church since childhood. He was taken into the fold after being found wandering alone along the beach near the monastery. He had been orphaned, but no explanations were found for his circumstances. He became a dedicated follower of the faith, and had remained with the church. He was over fifty years old now, but his exuberance was unabated.

Brother Benjamin was the nervous one of the group. Older than Ahira, he was cautious about his future well-being. He was not anxious to put himself at risk and was displeased with the prospect of having to face a nest of magicians in his own home.

Brother Pagiel was the last member of the council of elders, and the youngest. Barely forty years old, this was the first crisis he was faced with.

After Brother David repeated his story to the council, he was dismissed from further discussion.

"I don't like this," said Brother Benjamin. "I think we should just tell them to go, and be glad to be rid of them."

"That's not acceptable, and you know it," responded Ahira. "Our mission is to eradicate magicians from the earth, and nothing less is acceptable."

"What would you have us do?" demanded Benjamin. "Kill them while they sleep? Or perhaps we should wake them, and demand they confess to being magicians."

The scorn in Benjamin's voice was undisguised as he strove to find a safe solution to the problem.

"They must be tested," said Jeremias, attempting to quell an argument before it began.

"I'm very sure they would be happy to submit themselves to our testing," said Benjamin with a sneer playing at his lips.

"Your sarcasm is not lost on us, brother," interjected Ezekiel. "But, it does not help us to solve the problem. Tested they must be, agreeable or not."

"I think we can all agree on that," said Pagiel. "Whether Brother Benjamin admits to it or not. The problem is how. How do we get them to submit to our testing?"

When that question they all were asking themselves was finally posed, they fell silent. There were no answers at hand. Even though the brother's beliefs were rigidly held, this set of circumstances had never arisen before.

The magicians of this age were aware of the hatred and superstition that plagued them. They very seldom traveled into an area where there would be danger. They were confident that their magical abilities were strong enough to protect them from any dangers that may arise, but it was against their nature to force confrontation.

Due to the magician's secretive lifestyle, the brothers from the Church of the Second Millennium had never been in the position of needing to conduct their test, at least not in their lifetimes.

"I have been giving the problem some thought," declared Jeremias. "Our holy book is clear on the subject. Our faith will see us through. Our faith will bind the magicians to our will."

"Yes, God will protect us, and make his will be done," agreed Ahira.

"Then it will be done," said Jeremias. "We five will go to the cells of the travelers. They will be forced to take the test.

"And may God have mercy on their souls!"

It was an hour later when the five elders finally reached the basement cells where Michael and his friends were sleeping.

On the outside of the doors were wooden braces, fashioned to hold a cross-bar that would effectively lock the travelers in their rooms. Each of the council members carried just such a cross-bar.

When the rooms were all secured, Jeremias sent the other members to awaken the rest of the church. He would stay to guard the cells.

From inside his cell, Everett could hear the preparations being made for their capture. He was not concerned because he was sure their magic could handle the situation.

It would not be he who saved them however; he would leave that to Michael. It was Michael who would need to be able to handle the danger at Acantha's keep, and this would be good learning ground for him.

Everett knew Michael needed to be able to think of solutions quickly, and implement them without hesitation. If he could not do that here, where the danger was minimal, they would not have a chance against Acantha. The brothers of the church abhorred magic, so naturally they would have none at their disposal. But Everett could help Michael out if he got in trouble.

Outside the door he could hear the other members arriving. The leader of the church obviously felt there was safety in numbers. Everett rose from the hard cot and waited for the door to be opened.

Jeremias felt better when the members of the church began to show. He did not believe they would have any real hold over the travelers, if they were magicians, until they reached the father of the church. But, he felt a certain anonymity being surrounded by his brothers.

He signaled for the braces to be removed from the doors, and the doors opened. He saw four of the travelers being roused from an uneasy sleep. The fifth traveler, the old man, was standing in the middle of the cell with a solicitous smile on his face.

"I heard all of the commotion out here in the hall. I had no idea that I would have so many visitors at one time."

The easy manner of the old man unsettled Jeremias. He was obviously baiting them. Why would the old man be so secure when faced with so many churchmen in the middle of the night?

The other four travelers had now groped their way out into the hallway. "What's going on here?" demanded Thomas.

"You have been accused of harboring magicians among you," stated Jeremias. "How say you?"

"Ludicrous," replied Everett.

"Accused by who?" asked Michael.

"That is irrelevant," answered Ezekiel. "I was suspicious when I brought you here. Now we must know. Are any of you of the accursed?"

"How very dramatic of you, Brother Ezekiel," said Everett. "But, to answer your question, no, none of us are accursed."

"I feel you are playing with words," said Ahira.

"I also believe that may be true," added Jeremias. "You will go with us to speak to the father of the church. He will decide the course of our actions."

He turned on his heels and began walking the hallway back to the stairs without looking to see if he was obeyed.

The brothers of the church parted to allow passage for the travelers. After just a moment's hesitation, Everett followed the church elder, the rest of the travelers coming behind. Michael and Sarah walked hand in hand, Michael's smile was an attempt to calm the fears he knew Sarah would be feeling.

Upon reaching the room used for devotionals, Michael and his friends were shown to one of the benches in front. The holy men filled the room behind them, effectively blocking any avenue of retreat.

Five minutes later the church became hushed, and the brothers in the back began to part to allow passage to a newcomer. From Michael's viewpoint he could not see who was arriving, but there was no doubt in his mind that this was the church father, the old man he had seen at the evening devotionals.

As the part in the crowd reached him, he saw that he was right. The ancient man was being carried in on the ornate chair he had sat upon earlier. There were four men carrying the chair, one grasping each leg. They were not laboring under their task, the old man was frail, almost skeletal; Michael did not believe he could weigh more than a hundred pounds.

The four men carried their revered leader to the platform in the front of the room. Turning him to face the church body, they set the chair down and left the platform.

Jeremias and the four elders joined the old man. After a brief conference, Jeremias lifted his head.

"It has been said that among you five, there are magicians. Once again I ask...How say you?"

Sarah looked nervously over at Michael and Everett. There did not seem to be concern evidenced in their faces, but she was sure that she, Thomas, and Oliver had more than enough feelings of concern to make up for their lack.

"I will say only that you and your church have no right to judge us," answered Everett.

"It is God that will judge you," replied Jeremias.

"Okay, Michael," whispered Everett. "It's up to you now. Here is your test. Get us out of this."

Michael looked at his teacher with wide, startled eyes. He wasn't equipped to handle a situation like this. He needed more training, he couldn't just make them all disappear and then reappear somewhere else. He didn't have that kind of control over the emerald.

"What do you expect me to do?" beseeched Michael.

"Handle it!"

"How?"

"That's up to you."

Michael looked over to his other three companions, and saw how they were relying on him. He looked at Sarah and saw the fear on her face. Fear and what else? Trust! It was the trust on her face that made it even more difficult for him.

He wanted to tell her not to trust him. There was nothing he could do short of destroying everyone in the building that opposed them.

He looked back at the elders on the platform, and in an even voice asked, "You invited us here. You offered us sanctuary. What do you want from us?"

"We want an answer."

"I'll be damned if you'll get one!" Michael had raised his voice nearly to a shout. He had been pushed too much the last few months, and was determined that it would stop.

The elders on the platform seemed to draw up to taller heights under their robes at Michael's damnation. All but Benjamin. He seemed to shrink from the implied threat.

"Very nice, Michael," said Everett, sarcasm dripping from his voice. "You sure got us out of trouble with that bit of diplomacy."

"Their evasion should be answer enough," said Ahira.

"Don't make them mad!" whispered Benjamin, furtively. "You don't know what they could do."

Jeremias looked with scorn at his fellow brother. "You will be tested," he said when he turned back to the travelers.

"You will be taken from here to the highest tower of the church. From there you will be cast over the side. It is nearly sixty feet from the ground. Those of you that are magicians will, of course, save yourselves from the fall; but not from us. Those of you that are not magicians will be taken to your rewards with God."

Sarah gasped as she heard the brother's plans for her. "What kind of test is that? Either way we will die! Is that how you solve the problem? You just kill anyone you believe may be a magician?"

"If you are innocent," Jeremias replied, "you will be rewarded in Heaven. Your death will be a blessing bestowed upon you."

"Don't do me any favors!" She looked to Michael with pleading eyes. "Michael, I want to leave this place, and I want to leave now!"

He surged to his feet and glared at the pious holy man on the platform. Perhaps Everett was right, that he had no knack for being diplomatic, but he did not believe diplomacy would work with this bunch of fanatics anyway.

"This has gone far enough!" he shouted. "We're leaving, and if you care for your precious church, you'll just get out of the way, and not try to stop us."

He turned to Thomas and Oliver. "Get the packs and meet us in the main hall."

As the pair came to their feet, the rest of the church kneeled. Michael could not believe they would be so fortunate that they would be allowed to leave just because of his demands.

He turned to the platform and saw that the four elders had knelt as well. The ancient man, however, was beginning to move. He glared at Michael as his hands ruffled inside his cloak.

From his cloak he pulled on ornate cross, encrusted with diamonds. As the ancient one continued to scowl at Michael, his bloodless lips moved silently.

The room filled with a rainbow of colors. Michael found that he was unable to move as the light surrounded him. His entire group had been frozen where they stood.

They were unable to move as the elders came to them from their platform. They remained frozen as the ancient man continued to glare at them, now with a cruel smile playing across his features.

The members of the church body surrounded them, lifting them to take them to the highest parts of the church. Everett was helpless in spite of his magical powers. Michael was helpless in spite of the emerald that he did not yet fully understand. His friends were helpless because of their normalcy.

They were bundled up like dirty laundry being taken outside to wash in the rain. On every side of them there was a crush of church brothers. Hands grabbed to help carry them through the narrow hallways. Hands lifted them over the stairs, always leading up. They were completely aware of their surroundings, and could feel the cool fresh ocean air on their faces when the brothers expelled them onto the roofs. They could see the stars shining overhead, waiting to claim them for eternity.

Once they were on the roof, out of the darkness, came the old man in the chair. He was still being carried by four of the brothers. They moved him over to where the captive travelers were being held.

He spoke in a raspy voice, barely heard. "I know what you think. And you are right."

Still holding the cross in front of him like a weapon, he waved Jeremias over to him. "It is time...let the test begin."

With grim determination Jeremias walked over to the edge of the roof. When he reached the very end he stopped to gaze at the hard ground beneath him. It was well over sixty feet, closer to one hundred.

He turned to the brothers that were holding Michael and his friends. With a brisk wave of his hand he called them to him.

"Do it," he said quickly.

Without ceremony the five travelers were hurled from the top of the church, with all of the church members crowding near the edge, trying to get a look at the bodies that would inevitably be smashed on the ground below.

Jeremias had acted too swiftly. The ancient leader of the church did not have time to prepare himself. His talisman was strong, but due to his advancing age he was no longer strong enough to control it effectively. He needed to be in sight of his spell or it would be broken. Jeremias had the travelers thrown from the roof before he could be moved to within sight of the crime. Now he was held captive in his chair, cut off from sight by the brothers grouped near the edge.

As Michael and his friends were tossed from the roof, the spell was broken. They tumbled end over end, limbs flailing in the empty air. From somewhere a startled cry escaped trembling lips.

Michael was quick to act, there was no time allowed to look for the best solution to their danger. With hard, strained concentration, he brought the emerald to life.

The shield he had erected in the Cruz Mountains once again surrounded them. Since they were not standing on the ground this time, the shield took the form of a complete sphere. They were floating to earth, encased in a giant emerald green bubble.

From the roof of the church came anguished cries, and quickly said prayers. Their worst fears had been realized – the travelers were magicians.

With fists raised over head, eyes afire with hatred, the churchmen swarmed from the roof and down the stairs to do battle with their unholy enemy.

CHAPTER 14

The bubble floated to earth as the brothers of the church clambered down the stairs. It was an unusually clear night. The myriad of stars reflected off the emerald green bubble. Michael waved his arms and the bubble disappeared with an audible pop. Unprepared for the release, the travelers rolled to the ground. Sarah was on her feet before any of the men.

"Come on! We've got to get clear from here. If that old man gets near us with that cross, we're done for!"

Michael had scant time to marvel at her take-charge attitude before he had to begin running to catch up with the others.

"Wait a minute!" he called when he caught up with them. "I can handle this, I'm a magician!"

"Fat lot of good that did us earlier, Michael," called back Oliver. "If you don't mind, I'd rather try to outrun them than rely on your power."

They continued running until they reached the beach. It extended for nearly a quarter of a mile to the north, but they arrived at the south end of the beach, where it began to merge with rough rock outcropping.

"To the rocks," called Thomas. "We can make a stand there."

The group dashed into the cover of the rocks. Everett was the last to arrive, running slowly, puffing and panting.

"Why didn't you just fly over, Everett?" asked Sarah as she peered around the rock outcropping. "I've seen you fly before."

"You haven't seen me fly, child," answered Everett between gasps for breath. "You have seen me float. That's all that I can do, float where the wind will take me. And right now the wind is blowing inland, towards the church. I would just as soon not be over there, thank you very much."

"You had better get your breath back in a hurry, old man," said Michael. "Here they come, and they're as mad as hornets."

Everett rolled to his knees and peeked from behind the rocks. "I don't see the old man yet, do you?"

"No," replied Michael. "It will probably take them some time to haul that chair down the steps and out here."

Forgetting the real or imagined powers of magicians, the brothers of the church were rushing down the dark beach toward Michael and his group. Nearly forty fanatical men, some carrying pieces of driftwood or rocks they had picked up for weapons,

The charging men were within fifty yards when Michael and Everett finally decided on a course of action. Both men came to their feet at the same time, Everett's arms pin-wheeling and Michael's held straight out in front of him. The concentration was evident on both of their faces.

As the church brothers ran at them, the sand from the beach began to swirl at their feet, first slowly but picking up speed. Soon the sand was blowing fiercely in their faces.

Some of the stronger members bent their heads into the storm and surged ahead. A scant ten yards from their goal they smashed up against an invisible wall, their heads snapped back from the impact and the brothers fell to the ground.

"Okay," said Michael. "We can go now. But, we still need to hurry."

"How long will that barrier hold, Michael?" asked Everett.

"Your guess is as good as mine. Five to ten minutes, I would guess."

"That's good," offered Thomas. "We can lose them in the dark."

They were nearly two miles south before they stopped to rest. They had tried to move quickly, but the rough conditions of this section of the coastline made travel difficult even at the best of times.

Even with the bright moonlight, vision was difficult. There were quite a few of the gnarled trees that were indigenous to this area, and the black shadows that they cast made the travel treacherous. The ground was littered with stones, large and small, that threatened to twist a carelessly placed foot.

"This place offers good cover, Michael," said Thomas, as they descended down a rocky embankment to a secluded cove with a small beach.

They sank wearily to the soft sand to catch their breath. It had been a hard journey through the darkness, and the group had received only a couple of hours sleep.

"I'm not sure I understand what happened back there," said Oliver as he leaned back against the rock embankment. Like the rest of the travelers, he was nearing exhaustion after the near tragedy.

"What's to understand?" asked Thomas. "That old wizard of theirs caught us when we weren't looking. Then they threw us from the top of their church. I think that's easy enough to understand."

"That's just what I mean!" replied Oliver, undaunted by Thomas' logic. "If they think magicians are devils, what was that old man doing there?"

"That should be obvious," answered Everett. "He is a rouge magician, hiding out where he would be least expected. That's what he meant when he leaned over and said 'I know what you're thinking, and you're right'. He has the members of the church convinced that his power is not magic, but the power of God."

"That's a fine line that he has drawn for himself," interjected Michael.

"True enough," said Everett. "But, he has obviously been very successful walking that line. He has lived long enough to become ancient."

Sarah had been walking around their small hidden beach while they had been talking. She approached to where the men were sitting and stared down at them with her hands on her hips.

"There is no wood here to make a fire," she said. "And if there was wood, you probably wouldn't allow one anyway. I thought you big brave men were going to protect me! Instead, here we are in the middle of the night, on a cold little beach, with no fire."

She leveled her best scathing look on them as she continued. "What's more, we don't have any of the supplies. We left them all back at the church. We didn't even have a chance to use any of them." With that she turned her back to them and walked the few steps that was necessary to take her to the far side of the cove.

The chastened men shared embarrassed glances with each other before Michael spoke. "What was that all about? I guess I had better go over and try to calm her down."

Everett put his hand on Michael's arm as Michael began to get to his feet. "I'm not sure she needs to be calmed down. This is a group effort, and her input is just as important as anyone else's. And, what's even more important, is that she is entirely correct."

"Yeah, you're right," added Thomas. "We've been treating her like a little girl that needs protecting, without giving her any opportunity to contribute."

"I'm as much to blame for that as anyone," said Oliver. "All her life I've been looking over her shoulder, not giving her a chance to fend for herself."

The four men looked over at Sarah's rigid back. They made a group decision without speaking. Michael climbed to his feet and walked over to her.

He stood next to her and they both watched the waves surge gently to shore, the moon casting gentle light on the water.

"How does one go about apologizing for stupidity?" he asked.

Sarah looked up at Michael's brilliant and smiling green eyes. They moved into each other's arms, Sarah rested her head on his chest. Nothing further needed to be said. When a short time later they returned to the makeshift camp, Sarah's ire had been forgotten.

"So, what do we do now?" she asked.

"I think the first order of business should be to get our supplies back," answered Everett.

"You aren't thinking of going back there, are you?" asked Oliver.

"No, of course not. Michael greatly needs to sharpen his abilities, and we need to be able to work as a group. So, we go back to magic."

Everett instructed his friends on what he expected from them. He sat the group on the beach, in a small circle. With hands linked, legs crossed in front of them, and eyes closed, they concentrated on the individual cells where they had been situated.

Each member was to specifically concentrate on where they placed the supplies in the cells. With the picture of the supplies in each of their minds, Michael and Everett worked their magic to transport the packs from the cells to the center of the group.

Deep inside the church, in the basement cells, the packs were where the travelers had left them. The elders of the church had immediately sent Brother Benjamin to the cells to watch over the supplies. Should the accursed magicians return for them, he was to notify the other church elders immediately.

But Benjamin knew why he was sent here. The others considered him to be weak, and so had banished him to the cells to keep him out of their way.

He wished those devils would attempt to return. He would show the others just how brave and reliable he was. Now that the confrontation was over, Benjamin had convinced himself that he was a fearless acolyte of the faith.

Benjamin was walking from cell to cell muttering to himself about the injustice of it all. He was now in the cell of the little old man that had been so cocksure of himself when the brothers had first confronted the group. He thought of how he would teach that old man a lesson if he could get a hold of him once again. With a sigh, he kicked the supplies that had belonged to the old man, then turned and sat on the pack.

In a matter of minutes the ground in the center of the group began to shimmer with a faint green glow. Suddenly the sand exploded upward in a rush, as it was displaced by the arriving supplies. Sitting on one of the packs, with mouth agape in shocked surprise and terror, was one of the church elders. The members of Michael's group had opened their eyes when they heard the explosion, and returned the startled church brother's open-mouth gaze.

The brother continued to stare at all the people in the circle as the sand returned to earth in a raining shower. His hood had fallen from his head, and Michael could see that it was Benjamin, the elder that had seemed to shrink in fear at Michael's earlier outburst.

The falling sand continued to pelt the man's bald pate as he slowly rolled his eyes back in his head. With a soft moan escaping his lips, Brother Benjamin fainted, falling backwards from the packs into Thomas' arms.

By the time Brother Benjamin came back to his senses, the circle had been broken, and packs stowed against the embankment.

Sarah was chosen to speak to the faint-hearted man in hopes that he would not feel as threatened.

"What were you doing sitting on the packs?" she asked softly, as she knelt down beside him.

"Ohhhhh....," he said.

"You have to help me if I'm going to help you. What is your name?"

"Ohhhhh....," he answered.

"My name is Sarah. We are not here to hurt you, you know. We are just passing through. All we want to do is continue our journey in peace."

"Then why did you bring me here?" he finally asked. "I was minding my own business and you ensorcelled me."

He looked quickly around the camp at the men, as though he feared he had said too much, perhaps offending the magicians.

"We didn't mean to bring you here," Michael told him. "We were just retrieving our supplies, you happened to be in the way."

"I didn't mean to get in your way," Benjamin whined. "I was instructed to guard your belongings. The other elders of the church felt I would not be a hindrance to them if they could keep me out of the way." He shuddered. "Now look at me! I've been captured by the Devil's minions. I'll probably be condemned to Hell for eternity!"

Brother Benjamin was nearly wringing his hands as he contemplated his dim future.

"We have no intention of harming you, or keeping you here," Michael assured him.

"Then what do you want from me?"

"We don't want anything from you," answered Everett, as he moved over to join the conversation. "We do have some questions that we would like answered, but you will be free to go whether you answer them or not."

Benjamin looked at his captors as though he could not quite believe that one of his lifelong enemies, a magician, would be willing to let him live after getting him alone.

"What? What do you want to know?"

"That old man in the chair, who is he?" asked Everett.

"Father Samuel? Well, he is the father of our church."

"We figured he was your leader," said Michael. "We wanted to know where he came from, and how long he has been at the church."

"He has always been at the church," answered Benjamin, with a quizzical look on his face. "When I say he is the father of our church, I don't just mean the leader, I mean he is the very founder of our religion."

Everett was taken aback with this revelation. His understanding was that the Church of the Second Millennium was founded around the time of the Magicians' War.

"How is that possible, Brother Benjamin? That would make him nearly two-hundred years old!"

"Yes," replied Benjamin, with chest visibly inflated. "It is the Power of God that makes it possible."

"For God's sake, man!" Thomas implored. "Can't you see that your church father is a magician? Even I can see that, and I hadn't been exposed to magicians until a couple of months ago."

Benjamin visibly flinched from Thomas' tone. Proud of his church father as he was, he was still badly frightened to be under the control of this nest of magicians.

"I have answered your question, may I please go now?"

"Michael, do you still remember the spell of forgetfulness that I taught you so many years ago?"

"Yes. By the time he gets back to his church he won't remember why he was outside."

After Benjamin was allowed to leave -- his memory of the last hour wiped clean – Michael cast a spell to hide their camp. Sarah was even given the benefit of her campfire, not the traditional wood fire she expected, but one of magic that burned smoke-free and warm.

The questions of where Father Samuel had come from, and why he had formed the church, would have to wait. Everett was enthralled by the thought of a rouge magician hiding among the people that hated magicians the most. He could scarcely believe the old man had been around since the Magicians' War.

He would need to seek an answer to this in the future. But more pressing matters were at hand. In the morning Michael's group would once again strike south.

CHAPTER 15

Feeling a need to be as far from the Church of the Second Millennium as possible, the decision was made to break camp at first light. By mid-afternoon they were over five miles away from the church. They had reached a rugged area of the coast that was heavily overgrown with foliage on the left side of the old road, and had steep rocky drop-offs to the ocean on the right.

After the storm of the previous day, the air carried a cleanliness they could almost taste. The ocean, nearly two-hundred feet below them, was a brilliant, clear blue. It was calm and smooth, more like a large pond than the powerful mass that it was.

They were forced to walk along the old coast road rather than along the shoreline as there were no beaches along this stretch of shore, only huge seaweed-encrusted boulders. The weeds were constantly sprayed by the waves that came crashing into rocks, making them treacherous to walk upon.

As they had only a couple hours of sleep to separate two full days of travel, the group was nearing exhaustion. They decided to take a lengthy rest break in a shaded spot along the road. The shade was not provided by natural vegetation, rather by what was left of an ancient metal box. Its former condition was barely recognizable. It was rusted nearly through, and was collapsing in upon itself, but was still substantial enough to provide shelter from the afternoon sun.

"As big as this is -- and you still say that it was one of the ancient's wagons that traveled the roads under its own power?" asked Thomas as he looked over the relic.

"That's right," answered Michael. "See that big lump of metal in front of the box? That's the part of the machine that powered it."

Thomas looked at the mass of neglected metal as he slowly shook his head in awe. "It's amazing what they were able to do."

"I'm more interested in what we are able to do," put in Sarah. "If we ran into such difficulty with a group of holy men, how do we expect to confront Acantha and survive? How do we even get into the keep in the first place?"

All eyes turned to Everett. He was reclining in the shade, head on pack with hands linked on his chest and legs sprawled in front of him. His eyes were closed as if he was asleep. He sighed and rolled his head in Sarah's direction.

"I can get us into the keep without detection," he said. "Most of the rest will have to be left to Michael."

"How?" asked Michael. "What am I supposed to do?"

"Improvise, lad. Improvise."

The group watched Everett, waiting for further information, however none was forthcoming. Everett had fallen asleep.

\*     \*     \*     \*     \*

"How, old man? How do you plan to get into my keep?"

Acantha was once again watching Michael and his friends through her magic bowl.

She had lost two slaves through replenishing the blood supply needed to keep the magic bowl active. They had died when she drew too much of their blood for the all-day and all-night vigil she had kept during the stay and escape by Michael's group from the church. Her next chore would be to secure replacements for the slaves that she had lost.

Leaving her tower laboratory -- one of the few times she had done so in the last couple of months – she went in search of one of her most trusted captives. Milo was in the kitchen on the ground floor of the castle. He had been a cook on one of the supply ships that passed up and down the coast. Acantha had captured him when his ship had put in for repairs near the castle. Repairs that were made necessary because of Acantha. She had caused the damage with her magic. She had been in need of servants, and rather than going in search of them, she greatly preferred that they come to her.

While the ship's crew was busy making repairs, Milo had just walked away as if in a trance. Which was exactly the case. Once Acantha had him in her power, he quickly became enraptured by her cold beauty. She no longer needed a trance to keep him by her side, but Acantha would take no chances. She had a faithful servant in Milo, and she was determined that he would not change his mind. She kept him enraptured with magic as well as her feminine ways.

"Milo!" called Acantha as she neared the kitchen.

He looked up as he heard his name called. A sly grin played at his lips as he anticipated serving his lady.

"Oh, shit!" exclaimed Milo's helper. "The bitch is coming here."

Without looking, Milo lifted the nearest available pan and back-handed his helper across the face. "That's no way to talk about our mistress," stated Milo, as his helper crashed to the floor unconscious.

Acantha flowed into the kitchen, to see Milo standing over the fallen man. He only had eyes for her, however, as she entered the room. With uncharacteristic mirth, she asked, "Have you been playing with your helpers again, Milo?"

"He was disrespectful, my lady."

"How charming of you to come to my rescue, Milo. You are the ever-faithful servant. You will be rewarded later, but first I have a chore that needs to be done."

Milo listened intently as Acantha told him about losing two slaves, and the need to replace them. She would use her magic to transport him to a remote and sparsely populated area in the north. Once there, he was to find two suitable replacements. She would once again use her magic to bring them back to the castle.

Following Acantha up the stairs to the laboratory, Milo found it disconcertingly difficult to concentrate on the errand he was to do for his mistress. All he could manage to do was stare at the womanly figure preceding him. She was wearing a very thin, clingy black dress that swayed and moved with every step she took. It must have been made from the very finest silk, because every time she passed in front of a sunlit window her body was silhouetted inside the transparent garment.

He was mesmerized by the movement of her buttocks as she climbed the steps in front of him. Like two wildcats fighting inside a bag, he told himself.

Watching her as he was climbing, rather than watching where he was going, caused the inevitable to happen. He caught his toe on the lip of one of the steps, and with a startled cry fell forward, painfully banging his shins as he fell.

"Really, Milo," said Acantha, as she smiled down at the prone man, "you must watch what you're doing."

Face beet-red from embarrassment, he pulled himself to his feet and limped after Acantha as she continued the climb. Upon regaining her laboratory, Acantha was once again consumed by the business at hand.

"Do you know exactly what is expected of you, Milo?"

Milo puffed his chest with his feelings of self-importance. "You want me to capture a couple of men for you. No problem there."

"No, I do not want you to capture a couple of men. I want you to find the men for me. I will be watching you, once you have found them I will bring them back here myself. Do you understand?"

"Yes, Mistress." Milo's chest had deflated when he heard the disapproval in Acantha's voice. "But, how are you going to know when I've found them," he persisted.

"For God's sake, Milo! Don't be stupid, just do as I said. You find them, I'll do the rest."

Milo did not have a chance to inquire further. With a disgusted frown on her face, Acantha made an intricate pass with her hands, and he was gone.

Milo was scrambling for a foothold as he suddenly found himself on a steep hillside covered with brush and fallen pine needles. He was losing the battle, and soon rolled head over heels down the hill. He came to a halt as he splashed into a creek-bed at the bottom. With arms rigid behind him, he propped himself up in the middle of the creek. He looked around in confusion as the water from his soaked hair flowed down his face.

He was not an impressive figure under the best of circumstances. Barely over five and a half feet tall, Milo had a pudgy little body, two chins, and cheeks so round they obliterated any hint of a jaw line. Now, sitting in the middle of the swiftly flowing creek, blowing like a beached whale, he looked like anything but an agent of the most dangerous magician alive. His menace was not physical danger, but rather his lack of concern for anyone's safety or benefit except his own. If this little soiree would ingratiate him to Acantha, he was all for it. To hell with the lives of others that it may wreck.

He stood up to retreat from the water and gain his bearings. He was at the bottom of a ravine, the area around him was heavily wooded. Everything was deep in shadow, hidden from the early afternoon sun. Deciding to follow the stream to the coast, he slogged along beside it, water draining from his boots as he walked.

It took less than an hour of walking before he heard the sound of a woodsman's axe. Crawling on his belly -- in an attempt to come as close to the man as possible, and still not be seen – Milo had approached to within a scant few yards of the woodsman before he could see him. Peeking around the base of a slender pine, Milo could see the man working. His shirt was off as he worked furiously, splitting small logs. He was middle-aged, but had the body and muscular structure of a much younger man.

"There's one," Milo said to himself. "Now all that remains is for Acantha to take him. Then all I have to do is find one more."

"My God, but you are stupid!" Acantha's voice burst into Milo's head so quickly that he immediately flattened against the ground in an attempt to hide, thinking that the woodsman was sure to have heard the outburst, and would be after him in an instant with his axe.

"Oh, will you get up, Milo? That lumbering great oaf over there can't hear me. My voice is inside your head, only you can hear me."

"Oh," replied Milo with embarrassment.

He crawled backwards until he was out of site of the woods-man. He made his way back down the ravine before resuming his hunt.

"Are you still there?" he asked. He was looking around the heavily wooded area as he waited for an answer.

"Yes, I am still here. Now will you get on with the task I have assigned you?"

"Sure. Sure, I will. But, what was wrong with the woodsman?"

Milo could almost believe he could hear Acantha sigh with exasperation.

"I want a servant, Milo. I want someone that will accept being enslaved to me without putting up a fight. I'm too busy to concern myself with revolt from my servants. That woodcutter was the hero type. I can't be bothered with someone like him. Now go and find me someone as pliable as you!"

Acantha released her mental hold on Milo so quickly that he reeled from dizziness. He leaned against a nearby tree until he re-gained his senses. His next encounter was more to Acantha's liking. As he neared where the small stream fed into the ocean, he saw two men and a small boy crossing the stream ahead of him. He came to a halt as soon as he spotted them, in the hopes that he would not be seen. But his passage was too clumsy, too noisy. The trio looked up almost as soon as Milo spotted them.

"Well, if they're what you want, take them so I can get out of here," he muttered to himself as the two men took a couple of steps toward him.

With a blinding red flash, the two men disappeared in mid-step. It was hard to tell who was the more surprised, Milo or the small boy that had been accompanying the two men. They both stood rooted where they were, staring at the empty spot that had so recently been filled by the two men. The two moved their stare to encompass each other. Milo put his hands on his hips, raised his head in a haughty gesture and smiled a cruel smile at the boy.

The boy's mouth dropped open as his eyes grew in equal proportion. Understanding was settling into the boy, as the fear and loss battled to consume him. Like most small boys, this one had a gangly body, with spindly arms and legs. The rough mop of brown hair standing on his head went by its own rules, not conforming to anyone's wishes. "What did you do with my father!" he screamed at the man in front of him.

Milo continued to smile cruelly at the boy, his only sign that he heard was a slight lifting of his already elevated chin.

The boy's rage defeated his fear as he ran at his silent tormentor. He paused in his charge long enough to collect a couple of hand-sized rocks from the stream bed. "What have you done with my father!" he cried again as he resumed his charge.

As he charged, he hurled one of the rocks in his hands at the man. The first rock whizzed over Milo's head, missing by mere inches. The second rock struck him full in the chest.

"Hey!" bellowed Milo in shock. "What are you doing?"

"What did you do with my father?" was all the boy was capable of saying as he stopped to pick up two more rocks.

Once again he began to charge at Milo. Choosing discretion rather than valor was Milo's normal response to trouble. So it was now as well; he turned on his heels and ran from the wildly charging boy.

As he began to run, the next rock struck him in the middle of the back.

"Ow!!" came the painful response.

The last rock came in seconds later. It struck him on the back of the head. Milo felt himself beginning to lose consciousness. With the darkness beginning to enfold him, he could feel his balance leave him as he started to fall.

He saw the floor of Acantha's laboratory rush up to meet him as the darkness took full control.

CHAPTER 16

Milo opened glazed eyes and saw the late afternoon shadows on the floor of Acantha's laboratory. He rolled over to his back trying to remember how he had gotten there. The last he remembered he was in the woods somewhere. There were men, a stream-bed...and a small boy. With the thought of the boy, it all came back to him. He moved his hand to the back of his head to massage the delayed pain that was living there. His hand came away sticky.

"Now, do you see what I mean when I say I don't want any hero types around here, Milo? I want them all to be just as cowardly as you."

He turned to find the body behind the voice, wincing at the pain his movement caused. He saw Acantha sitting at her work bench. She was posed on a heavy wooden chair. Her legs were crossed, one arm was casually flung over the back of the chair; the other was resting on the bench, fingers tapping in rhythm.

"But, coward or not, you accomplished the task I set before you. Now," she continued, "we shall attend to the reward I promised you earlier. If you feel that you can raise yourself from the floor, you may lead me to my chambers."

Milo painfully clambered to his feet. The grin that threatened to split his face in half belied the throbbing hurt in his head. He rushed for the door, looking over his shoulder to see if she was following him. He would be her lap dog for a few hours; that's all he had hoped for.

Acantha allowed her own grin to play across her face; this fool would be her source of amusement. Even world conquerors needed their time of decadence. She rose to follow the pudgy little man to her private rooms. There would be time enough later to concern herself with Michael and his foolish friends.

*    *    *    *    *

While Milo had been on his hunt, Michael's group had spent the entire time overlooking some of the most rugged scenery the west coast could produce. About the time Acantha took Milo to bed, they had once again begun their journey south. Little progress was made throughout the late afternoon. This area of the coast -- as well as the next fifty miles – was the most difficult to traverse. The coast road they had been following was nearly destroyed along most of the route. What did remain was dangerous to travel because of the decaying conditions next to the rock-strewn drop-offs. Only a handful of miles could be completed in a day's travel before exhaustion would once again set in.

Camp was made that night on a grassy knoll right at the edge of one of the cliffs. Nature put on a dazzling display for their benefit. The western sky was aflame in shades of orange and lavenders. The curve of the ocean's horizon reflected the colors back to the sky in mirror-like images. The five silhouetted forms sat on the knoll, experiencing the sight before they set about starting the evening fire. The day's journey had been rough and they were enjoying the chance to rest before beginning the evening's activity.

"How long before we reach Acantha's keep, Everett?" asked Sarah.

"Oh, a month if we hurry. A month and a half if we don't."

"Are we in a hurry?" asked Thomas.

Everett smiled at his mammoth friend before answering. "No, not yet anyway. I don't want to show up before Michael is ready. And he is woefully short of being ready yet."

"Well, I don't know what you think is going to happen in the next month -- or month and a half, as far as that goes – that is going to prepare me," Michael replied.

"Really, Michael," answered Sarah in exasperation. "He wants you to experience what the emerald can do. He wants you to use your abilities every chance you get so they will get stronger."

Everett looked with surprise at the girl he had so easily dismissed not many days earlier. She was showing an intelligence and understanding for the situation that he had previously thought was beyond her capabilities.

"I could not have put it better myself, Sarah," he said. Turning to the rest of the travelers, he added, "She is absolutely correct. This has been a rough trip so far, and it's going to get worse, the nearer we get to our goal. Acantha will use greater force the closer we get, and you will need to call on strength greater than you knew was possible."

Michael stood with a sigh that signaled he felt he was carrying the weight of the world on his shoulders. "Well, I'm glad that you feel..."

Michael's words were cut off by a low rumbling sound that was rapidly becoming a roar. Vibrations from the ground could be felt by the travelers. The deafening roar and shaking of the ground likened to an earthquake without the rolling motion.

"What the hell's going on?" shouted Oliver as he lurched to his feet.

"I think the cliff-face is giving way!" shouted Thomas.

The three that were still sitting now jumped to their feet, grabbing the packs that contained supplies that could not be replaced in this remote area. They began to make a dash as far from the cliff face as they could, hoping to reach safety in distance.

Everett, Sarah, and Oliver were the farthest from the drop, and were steps ahead of Michael and Thomas when tons of rocks from the side of the cliff erupted upwards as though spewed from a miniature volcano.

"Magic!" was all Michael managed to shout before one of the flying rocks delivered a glancing blow to his head.

In two powerful strides, Big Thomas rushed to the fallen Michael. He scooped him up in his arms and threw him over one shoulder without pausing to check his condition.

"Run! I've got him! Run!"

Everett, Sarah, and Oliver turned and continued the panicked retreat. Rocks, boulders, even small pebbles continued to vomit skyward. The rubble was flying a hundred feet or more into the air before beginning to rain down among the travelers.

Everett managed to hastily erect a magical shield covering their retreat, but the massive blows that were being hammered down on them were weakening Everett. His strength was beginning to fail him as the onslaught began to slow, finally coming to a halt with the smaller pebbles and dirt showering down in an anticlimax. The three finally stopped their run to gaze about them in disbelief. The ground between them and the grassy knoll where they had been resting was strewn with rocks and boulders of all sizes. Michael and Thomas were nowhere in sight.

*     *     *     *     *

Thomas had hauled Michael from the ground and begun running with him as the first of the upward avalanche struck. Because of the darkness, the panic, and the sky full of rocks and boulders, Thomas was unclear of which direction to take. The truth be told, he did not pause to consider where he should run. He just ran in the direction he was headed.

As he ran parallel to the edge of the cliff, the contour of the land herded him closer to the edge. A large boulder came crashing down within feet of him. It was just to his left, and he instinctively veered to the right, closer to the edge. The path he was following began a gradual descent, but soon, the angle of decline increased. He found himself careening nearly out of control, afraid to slow his speed for fear of losing his grip on Michael. Everything was becoming a blur to him, Michael was bouncing heavily on his shoulder, rocks were flying in a maelstrom around him, whizzing past his right shoulder as he flew down the side of the cliff.

One instant he was charging down, the ground jolting his body with each out-of-control step, the next instant there was nothing. He found himself in mid-air; everything was silent as he began to somersault into a void. The pressure of his fall nearly tore Michael loose from his grasp. With a bone-jarring impact, his fall was over. Thomas drifted away from consciousness with the sound of the surf slapping the shore.

Everett, Sarah, and Oliver began to retrace their route back to the edge of the cliff-face. They proceeded slowly, with caution in case the earth should disgorge more of its rubble their way.

"God, you don't think they're under one of these boulders, do you?" asked Oliver.

"I don't know. I just don't know," answered Everett.

"Which way did they run?" inquired Sarah. "Can you find them with your magic, Everett? Can't you sense them or something?"

Everett's head swung from one end of their grassy rest area to the other, amazed at the destruction. He shook his head from side to side. It was not clear whether he was answering Sarah, or was contemplating the power it must have taken Acantha to unleash this latest attack.

"I don't know, Sarah. I can't reach Michael at all. I just don't get anything in return. I don't know if he is under one of those rocks, or if he is hurt somewhere. I just don't know."

"Well, let's look for them!" Sarah was nearing panic from the thought of losing Michael.

"Don't worry, Sarah, we'll find them," said Oliver as he moved to put a protective arm over her shoulders. "But it is beginning to get quite dark. In a matter of minutes we'll lose all hope of finding them tonight."

"Well, let's get to it," called Everett as he moved carefully to the edge of the drop-off. Peering over the side he saw it was already too dark to even see the rocky beach at the bottom.

"I wonder if there are any rocks left down there at all," he murmured to himself.

They searched well into the night, but there was no hope they would be able to find any trace of the missing pair in the darkness. If they were not careful they would get separated themselves. Eventually it became necessary to call a halt to the search until morning. With spirits low, they hunkered down around a meager fire to wait for first light.

CHAPTER 17

When dawn finally broke, Everett, Sarah, and Oliver had already been looking for Michael and Thomas for nearly an hour. The night's rest was fitful at best, and they finally gave up trying to find sleep. They had searched around the larger boulders for any signs of clothing or human remains, hoping they would find none. After completing an exhaustive search of the surrounding area, they began looking for a way down to the shoreline, some one hundred feet below them. Unfortunately, they were searching toward the north; the route Thomas had chosen was toward the south.

"Do you sense anything yet, Everett?" asked Oliver.

"If I did, I would lead you straight to them!" snapped Everett. "I'm sorry, that's not fair of me. I know we are all concerned."

Sarah touched his arm tenderly, trying her best to console him, even though she was consumed with fears of her own.

"We understand, Everett. We're all on edge right now. We'll just have to keep looking."

\*     \*     \*     \*     \*

Nearly a half mile to the south, Thomas was just beginning to stir. He was lying face down upon the sand, in a small cove that had been hidden from above. There was a sharp pain in his chest, and he feared he had broken ribs from the fall he had suffered the night before.

Carefully he rolled to his side to take inventory of what might still be functioning. As he slowly and painfully gained a sitting position, he saw his hunting bow broken into three pieces, lying in the sand where he had just been.

"Damn," he cursed, silently, "I wish it had been my ribs."

Finding the rest of his body in an unbroken -- if somewhat painful – state, he began to remember the events leading up to the fall.

"Michael," he said weakly, as he remembered carrying him from the magical avalanche, and then the fall with Michael still over his shoulder. Even as he was remembering, he was turning to look for his friend. He saw Michael's unmoving form a mere ten feet behind him. Slowly, hampered by a myriad of small and large aches and pains, Thomas staggered to his feet and limped over to where Michael sprawled on the sand. As he kneeled down next to him, Thomas could see Michael's face was crusted with dried blood. Whether it came from the rock that had struck him, or from the fall, Thomas could not tell.

Since his own clothing was made entirely from leather, Thomas tore a strip of cloth from Michael's shirt. This he took to where the waves were gently rolling to shore. He returned to Michael's side with the wet cloth and began cleaning the dried blood from his face. Hopefully he would be able to see the extent of the damage once the crusty brown mess was removed. What he would do if the damage was extensive was beyond concern at the moment.

Michael began to groan in pain as the cold water began to bring him back to his senses. He continually tried to push Thomas' hand away as his friend was cleaning his face. When he finally began struggling to a sitting position, Thomas put one of his massive arms gently behind him to help, should weakness prove to be too much for Michael's efforts.

"Do you enjoy inflicting pain on helpless people," asked Michael, with a scowl.

"Huh?" responded Thomas.

"Salt water. You were rubbing salt water into what feels like a hundred cuts on my face. Stung like hell!" grumbled Michael.

Thomas grinned through his sand-encrusted beard as he sat upon his haunches. "Well, at least it worked. You're back to your usual likable self."

Michael reached for Thomas' shoulder as an aid, as he carefully pulled himself to his feet. "Where the hell are we, and what happened?" he asked quietly and looked around.

"Well...where we are is easy, we're at the bottom of the cliff that we stopped at last night. What happened ain't so easy to answer." As Thomas recounted what had happened, Michael staggered to the water's edge, and into the ocean to knee depth. Once there he scooped handfuls of the frigid water into his face, wincing at the needle-like stabs of pain.

Once he had completed his story, Thomas asked him, "Why is it that you can rub that salt water in your face, but you hollered bloody murder when I was trying to clean you up?"

"Believe me, Thomas, I'm no happier with my doing it than I was when you did."

He stopped his banter with Thomas as he realized they were alone. He began to look around him with real concern.

"Where is everyone else? Where's Sarah?"

The big man turned his eyes from Michael, not wanting to admit he could not answer his question without causing Michael more pain.

"Don't know, Michael. I hollered for them to run. The last I saw, they were making a hasty retreat inland. I just don't know for sure what happened to them."

"Help me to shore, Thomas. If I can get my wits about me, I should be able to track Everett through our bond of magic."

Almost ten minutes later Michael had composed himself enough that he was able to locate his teacher. He told Thomas not to worry, that Everett had located them through his own magic, and that all three were now on their way to rejoin them.

It was nearly a half hour before Everett, Sarah, and Oliver made their way back to the previous night's resting place, and then found the path down to the beach where Michael and Thomas waited.

Sarah nearly knocked Everett from the path in her haste to reach the bottom. Once on the beach, she rushed to Michael and the greeting of his open arms.

"Oh, I thought I had lost you for good this time," she cried. "Look at your face," she continued, as she peered up at his bruised and battered smiling face. "How did you get down here, anyway?"

"Thomas can answer that better than I can. I was unconscious almost from the beginning."

"Not until I take care of those cuts!" she said. She promptly tore a strip of cloth from her shirt and dashed to the water.

"Oh, no," groaned Michael, looking over to Thomas. "More salt water!"

The travelers used the rest of the day to regain their strength. They discussed how best to proceed with their travel plans and the attack to come on Acantha's keep, intermingling the serious matters with small talk about things they had done before they had met.

As Sarah sat and listened to the exploits of the men in their past, she thought back to the loss of her uncle nearly a year ago. Feeling an unusual camaraderie with these worldly men, she recounted the story of her loss.

"We always supplied our own meats for the tavern's tables," she said. "Uncle Gus would go into the hills behind the village for a couple of days to do his hunting when supplies would begin to run low. He always took a couple of the men from town with him. They would need to provide food for their own table, plus they felt there was safety in numbers."

Sarah paused in telling her story, remembering the grief and pain she had felt upon learning how her beloved uncle had died on his last hunting trip. She scooped handfuls of the dry sand, and watched it slip through her hands, like the happiness that had slipped away from her a year ago.

"Well," she continued, "he took a couple of his regular hunting friends with him on this last trip. You know Pete and Larry, don't you Oliver?"

"Oh, sure. I remember that day very well, child."

"Yes," said Sarah quietly. "Anyway, they had gone looking for deer, but felt they had an added bonus when they ran into fresh boar tracks. Ham steaks, bacon, and pork chops are always a welcome addition to a tavern's fare. Uncle Gus and his two friends began tracking the boar. They were pretty far up into the hills, heading toward a stream bed. They figured that's where they would find the wild pig. Before they got to the stream, they heard scrabbling in the brush off to one side of the trail. They notched arrows as the rustling got closer. All of the men were faced toward the sound in the brush.

"Suddenly from behind them -- from the opposite side of the trail – an enraged boar charged from under the cover of heavy brush. There must have been two of them. The one that charged came right at my Uncle Gus. He barely had time to turn and see what was happening when it struck. The boar knocked him down and with his tusks ripped a large hole out of his stomach before Pete and Larry could put arrows in it. It took three arrows to stop the damn thing.

"Anyway," Sarah concluded, with a deep sigh, "Uncle Gus died before they could get him back to town."

"Practically the whole town turned out for his burial, I might add," said Oliver. "He was well loved, and has been greatly missed."

Sarah's story made the travelers reflect upon all that had been lost in the past, from Sarah's Uncle Gus to Michael's parents and all of Everett's life-long friends.

As evening approached, the travelers gathered what driftwood was dry enough to start a small campfire. Sarah and Michael were gathering the wood when Michael broached the subject about her uncle.

"You've never told me the entire story about your uncle's death before," said Michael, as he bent to pick-up a small piece of wood.

Sarah smiled shyly at Michael and stooped to grasp a long whip-like portion of kelp that had washed to shore. Watching the trailing end of the whip as she slowly swung it from side to side, she spoke to Michael about the loss she had suffered, and her fears of further loss.

"It still hurts, you know," she said softly. "He was everything to me, and I lost him so quickly. I didn't even have a chance to tell him I loved him one last time. Then, when we couldn't find you this morning, I thought of how I didn't want to go through that again."

She carelessly tossed the strand of kelp to the ground, and looked out at the darkening ocean before turning back to Michael. "I love you so much, Michael. What you're planning to do is dangerous, so very dangerous. I don't want to lose you, not ever."

Michael let the few pieces of driftwood fall from his hands as he moved to embrace Sarah. He stood briefly holding her, one hand behind her head with fingers intertwined in her hair, welcoming the feel of her body next to his, matching her breathing with his and feeling as one.

He whispered into her ear. "You won't lose me, Sarah, because that would mean I would lose you as well, and I won't allow that. I will learn all there is to learn, all that Everett can teach me about controlling the emerald. And I will do whatever it takes to defeat Acantha."

Later, with the small campfire lit, the group sat or reclined in near silence. Michael and Sarah were lying in the sand, staring at the canopy of brilliant stars overhead. Everett and Thomas were speaking quietly near the fire. Oliver was sitting alone on the opposite side of the fire, staring into its flames as though hypnotized.

"Why so quiet, Oliver?" asked Everett when a gap in his conversation with Thomas appeared.

"Hmm? What?" asked Oliver, as he slowly pulled his gaze from the fire.

"You've hardly said two words all evening. What's on your mind?"

"Oh, I was just thinking about how hard the trip south is going to be. The terrain is getting rougher all the time. I understand why you don't want to go by boat – we'd be stuck out in the open if Acantha attacked. But, I still think with all the talent here, there must be an easier way. After all, our ancestors were smart enough that they figured a way to get from place to place without walking. Why can't we?"

"Well, I'm used to walking through the mountains," said Thomas, "but, if you've got any ideas that will make it any easier, I'm for it."

Everett propped his arms on his knees as he sat forward toward Oliver. "Have you been thinking of something specific, Oliver? I may be an old teacher of magic, but that does not mean I'm too old for new ideas."

Oliver leaned to one side, resting on his left arm, his right hand stroking the coarse stubble of his unshaven face. "Well, I was thinking of what Michael said back in the Cruz Mountains, about people flying through the air in machines. He said that was in the old days before magic came to the world."

Michael rose from lying on his back. Now in a sitting position he spoke to Oliver. "That was using a science that is lost to us now, Oliver. It's a feat we will never be able to duplicate again."

Oliver shook his head, and waved Michael's objection away with his hand. "I'm not so sure, Michael. I was also thinking of a couple nights ago, when we were escaping from those mad church-men. Sarah asked Everett why he didn't fly, and he said all he could do is float where the wind took him."

Oliver was beginning to become animated with the excitement of his unprecedented idea. He straightened back up to an upright position and leaned into the fire, to reach closer to the magicians upon whom rested the success of his idea.

"Everett, can you make other things around you float, like this piece of wood here?" At this point he grasped a peace of driftwood that was set aside for when the fire burned down.

"Of course," responded Everett. "It's a simple trick really, just a matter of displacement."

"Could you lift a large, heavy piece of wood?" continued Oliver.

"Well...within limits, of course."

Oliver's attention returned to the flames of the fire, once again lost in his thoughts.

"What are you getting at, Everett?" asked Sarah, as she stood to move over to his side of the fire.

"I don't know, wishful thinking maybe," he said as he continued to stare into the fire.

"I think I begin to see where you're going with this, Oliver," said Everett into the silence. "If you lashed enough wood together for three or four people to sit on, Michael or I either one could easily make it float. But, that wouldn't do us any good. We would just sit in the air and float, we would be too heavy for the wind to push us anywhere."

"Not if I rigged up a sail, like on my fishing boat! Remember, I lived my whole life on the ocean, I'm sure I could build the vessel that would harness the wind, if you could keep it in the air."

Everett sat in silence, considering Oliver's idea. He looked over at Michael and raised his eyebrows in question. He was answered by Michael's raised shoulders. He was as perplexed as Everett.

"I don't know, Everett," Michael said. "Just because it's never been done before doesn't mean it won't work."

Everett rose from the sand and paced back and forth in front of the fire. "I have no idea if this air vessel of yours will work, and I fear it's all academic anyway. Granted, you and Thomas could surely build the vessel, but what would you use for the sails?"

Oliver seemed to deflate in front of Everett's questioning eyes. "I don't know, I haven't thought it all out yet. I said it might all be wishful thinking, but it's not an idea I want to let go of right now."

"Well, when you figure it out," replied Everett, "let me know, but for tonight I'm done speculating. It's time to sleep."

The rest of the travelers soon followed Everett's example. All but Oliver who stayed up well into the night, thinking and rethinking an idea that he was certain would work.

CHAPTER 18

A week later Michael and his group of travelers were in a very heavily wooded area of the coast. It was some of the most rugged and overgrown area they had been in yet. They had moved a good distance inland as they traveled, and now walked among intimidating stands of tanbark oak trees and giant redwoods.

Late summer showers had followed them for most of the last week. The mountainous area they had moved into was quickly becoming choked with the lush ferns that would grow taller than their heads.

Finding it nearly impossible to traverse through the bracken and fallen rotted trees that were covered with a coating of slick moss, they finally gave up the idea of traveling inland and began moving at a slow rate back to the rocky shoreline.

"Now, see what I meant about flying? If we could rig up one of those flying boats I was talking about, we could just sit comfortable and fly above all this stuff instead of trying to push our way through it."

Oliver had been retelling his idea of a flying boat repeatedly over the course of the last week. The other travelers at first thought it a very sensible idea, if they had been able to acquire the materials necessary to make the sail.

Eventually, however, after hearing of Oliver's flying boat night and day, their enthusiasm had bled dry.

"Oliver, we love the idea of your silly flying boat," groaned Thomas. "But, we don't have one, and we don't have the means or materials to make one. So hush up about it, and keep walking!"

"Yeah, I hear you," replied Oliver as he pushed his way past an unusually large fern that crossed the animal path they were following. "And if you weren't so damned big I'd...

"Wait a minute," interrupted Everett.

The entire group stopped as they saw Everett gazing down the ravine that ran along their path.

"What do you see?" asked Michael as he followed Everett's gaze.

"A wisp of smoke. I saw a wisp of smoke through the trees up ahead."

The travelers all stared toward where Everett was pointing. No smoke could be seen now, but the wind could have blown it in another direction.

Michael had been practicing his magic at every opportunity the past week, so it surprised no one when he began to lift off the ground. He passed the twenty foot level that Everett was used to floating at, and kept rising. Nearly fifty feet from the ground, Michael stopped his ascent and hung motionless in the air.

He pointed to the area Everett had said the smoke came from, and began saying something to his friends; but, at that level the sound of his voice was lost in the trees.

Everett raised his hands, palms up, to the level of his shoulders to indicate they could not hear him. Michael began to lower himself when he realized he could not be heard.

The wind had blown him some feet from where he was standing, and more than once in his descent he had to push himself away from branches of trees, either with his hands or feet.

Sarah reached up to his hands as though helping him as he settled to the ground. Once firmly down, Sarah pulled him to her in a strong embrace. Although it was no longer a surprise to see him use his magic, Sarah felt that they were drawn further apart with each occurrence. She had never been exposed to any magic in the past, and Michael's powers were growing at an increasing rate. In her mind, the rift that was growing between them was caused by the visible change in Michael. While he changed and grew daily, she felt that she was not keeping up; that she was still the naive little girl that had never been out of the small village of Monterey. She did not stop to think of the changes in herself; changes that the others were noticing daily.

No longer did they have to slow their travels to her pace, she kept up with whatever demands were made of her. She had traveled more in the past few weeks than most grown men. On at least three different occasions she had survived life threatening situations, and still she pressed ahead.

She was not aware of these changes in herself, but they had not gone unnoticed by her fellow travelers. Michael watched her blossom into a mature, capable woman, and felt a pride that he had never felt for another person.

"What did you see, Michael?" she asked when she finally released him from her hold.

"Just as Everett said. The smoke you saw, Everett, is from a shack just ahead. There is a stone chimney along the near wall of the shack. Whoever lives there has a fire going."

Everett nodded his head in response to Michael's report. Looking up at the level of the sun in the sky, he answered Michael. "Yes, it's early evening now. People in this area are in bed with the sun. They are probably preparing dinner."

"Dinner!" interjected Thomas, with a smile. "What are we waiting for?"

"Yes," continued Everett, "we must not keep your stomach waiting. But, we will go with caution. We do not know who lives in that cabin; and they most certainly will not be expecting us."

The five of them continued their way through the lush forest. Nearly a half-hour later they approached the small cabin. It was solidly made, using logs cut from the oak trees that had strangled the path that Michael and the others had been following. There were two open windows along the front of the cabin, none on the sides. Glass was not readily available to people that lived in the wilderness, so Michael assumed they would have shutters that swung in toward the interior of the cabin, and could be secured at night.

As they came closer to the cabin, it appeared there were two people standing on the covered porch. With Sarah in the lead, to calm the inhabitants that may be fearing an attack by strangers, they moved close enough to the two people on the porch to recognize that one was a middle-aged woman, the other a small boy, perhaps ten years old.

"Ya' just stop right there!" called the boy. As he called his warning to the approaching strangers, he pulled a length of sturdy oak from behind his back. The hardened oak club was nearly as long as the boy was tall, and as thick as Big Thomas' forearms. He had to use both hands to keep the club under control.

"If yer part of them what took my dad, ya'd better spit out what ya' done to him! If yer not, ya' best be high-tailin' it outta here!"

Taking lead of the group, Sarah raised her hand to stop the men. "Let me talk to them. Maybe they won't feel threatened by a woman."

She put on her best smile as she continued walking toward the cabin. The small boy seemed to be uncertain what to do now that one of the strangers failed to heed his warning. He turned to look up at the woman that stood on the porch with him, as though seeking advice. The woman, however, just stood on the porch, wringing her hands, watching the approach of the unknown girl.

Rightfully assuming that he would get no help from the woman, the boy turned back to the stranger. He tried mightily to stand taller and puff out his chest before he spoke.

"Ya' stop right there, lady. I ain't got no reason not to bash in a lady same as I would a man."

Sarah bravely continued to approach the couple until she was within ten feet of them. There she stopped and once more smiled at the small boy.

"You have nothing to fear from us. We are traveling south, and just happened upon your cabin. We have been sleeping in the open for weeks, and hoped we would have a chance to have a roof over our heads tonight. We would gladly do whatever work you need done here to pay for the privilege."

The boy once more looked back at the woman. The woman was looking from Sarah to the men that waited some distance away, and back to Sarah again.

Moving to place a protective arm around the boy, the woman finally broke her silence. "My name is Esther, this is my son, Brian. You and your friends are welcome here."

"But, Mom!" interrupted the boy as he twisted around to look up at the woman by his side.

"Now, son...we can't live in fear, and maybe these folks can tell us something about what happened to your dad."

Sarah turned and called her friends to her. When they were together in a group again, Sarah introduced each in turn.

Esther, over the strident objections of her son, invited the travelers into her home. She offered them small helpings of the stew she had been preparing. With apologies for the meager fare, she explained how her husband and his brother had been stolen by a wizard, and her supplies had been dwindling since her loss.

"...and after Brian chased the wizard, throwing rocks at him, the wizard disappeared."

"A tragedy, no doubt about that," offered Everett, "but I don't think this man was a magician. I think he was controlled by a magician. If he had been one himself, he could have easily protected himself from a few thrown rocks."

Everett told Esther about Acantha, and his belief that Acantha was behind the taking of her husband and brother-in-law. After gaining the trust of Esther and her son, he told them of the quest to regain the magical ruby. The promise was made to give every effort to gain the release of her husband and his brother.

Michael and the boy, Brian, stayed up into the night, past the time when everyone else was asleep, talking about the good and evil in magic. Michael felt it was necessary that the boy learn that there was good and evil in the world, and that it affected all areas of life, not just magicians.

The next morning dawned bright and warm, a welcome change after the last week's rainstorms. Everyone was doing their part in helping Esther finish the chores that had piled up since the loss of her husband. Sarah and Esther had left early to do the laundry at the stream bed close by. Big Thomas and Oliver were on a hunt to supply

Esther's dwindling larder. Thomas was given the loan of one the hunting bows that belonged to Esther's husband. It did not have the stiffness that Thomas favored because of his size and strength, but it was a sturdy, well-made weapon nevertheless. That left Michael, Everett, and Brian to chop a good supply of wood for the cool evenings, and for cooking.

Michael was perspiring heavily under the early sun as he swung the head of the axe in yet another whistling arc. Once a log was cut into manageable sized pieces, Brian would rush in to grab an armful and then retreat to stack it neatly against the cabin.

"So, if yer a magician, Michael," the boy said, as they both stopped to catch their breath, "why don't ya' cut and stack all this wood using magic. It'd sure be a far sight easier."

Michael smiled down at the boy as he wiped the sweat from his face with his hand. "Yes, it would be easier at that. But, then I would become fat and lazy. That was one of the things my teachers tried to teach me early; don't use magic to get out of work that can be done easily by hand. Man's nature is to take the easy way out. That's not always the best way."

Brian considered Michael's words before responding.

"Yeah, well if I was a magician, I'd just sit back and wave my hand and get everything done."

"Well, perhaps that's why you're not," replied Michael gently.

Brian scowled up at Michael. "Ya' mean 'cause I'm lazy I can't do magic?"

Michael laid his ax down and sat on the cutting block to take a rest and speak with the young boy.

"No, I don't believe you're lazy. I've watched you stack that wood for the last hour. I mean you lack the respect of magic, it's not a toy to be played with."

"But this Acantha lady doesn't respect it, does she?" he asked.

"Not anymore, I'm afraid. But she did when she learned."

"Do ya' think if I respected it, I could learn?" the wide-eyed Brian asked.

Michael ruffled the boy's hair as he stood. "I'm sure you could. Now let's get back to work."

Over lunch the talk turned once more to Oliver's flying boat. "You may be right, Oliver," said Everett. "Now may be the time to build your vessel; that is if Esther could be convinced to part with her curtains."

Esther jumped at the chance to be of help, if it would hasten these adventurers on their way to her husband's rescue. "Not only would I give my curtains to your quest, but I will sew them myself to fit your needs."

"You just tell me what you need as a base for this ship of yours, Oliver, and I'll chop down as many trees as we need," offered Thomas, anxious to do his part in this grand scheme.

"I don't want to try to float half the forest, make it as small as possible," said Everett.

"I don't think we need that much," agreed Oliver, "just a couple of planks to sit on, and a pole or two to rig the sail on."

"Well then, let's finish lunch and get to work," said Sarah. "I'll help Esther with the sails, and you men can go out and work up another sweat."

With everyone pitching in to help, all of the materials were at hand by nightfall. The actual construction would wait until first light. The remainder of the evening would be spent around the fire in light conversation. Off in one darkened corner of the cabin, Michael sat alone. With legs crossed and hands clasped in front of him, he was lost deep within a meditating trance.

Brian, awed with the unknown power of magic, crept from the fire to sit in front of Michael, watching over him protectively. He would shortly get his first taste of the true potential of magic.

CHAPTER 19

Michael sat in the trance, oblivious to his surroundings. He was not aware of his friends sitting by the fire, and he did not realize that Brian had moved over to sit in front of him. He was lost within his mind, searching for the limits to the emerald's power, and for the ways to tap them.

Over the past few weeks of the trip, with each period of meditation, Michael gained more knowledge and understanding of what was necessary to call upon the potential of the emerald. The same was true on this occasion. He reached out with his mind and grasped what he saw as new tendrils of knowledge.

Behind his closed eyelids, he began to see light filtering through. The light began to dissolve into shapes and forms. With his eyes still closed, Michael first saw Brian sitting directly in front of him, intently watching for any miraculous occurrences. Rising a couple of feet, he could see Sarah, Everett, Oliver, and Thomas sitting by the fire, talking quietly. Occasionally Everett or Sarah would glance over to where Michael sat. Seeing no difference in his posture, they would then turn back to their conversation.

Not understanding why they had not noticed that he had risen from a sitting position, Michael moved closer to the fire and his friends. Sarah once again turned to glance at Michael. Seeing him still sitting in the corner, she once again turned back to the fire. Confused, Michael turned to look into the corner that he had just left. Sitting there was Brian, intently watching a slender dark-haired man in meditation.

"Good Heavens, that's me," thought Michael.

Looking down to where he should be standing, he saw only blank floor. He was terrified of the thought of being trapped outside of his body. Quickly he floated back, and found that he could easily re-enter. He opened his eyes and seeing Brian sitting in front of him, offered the small boy a private smile. When the smile was returned,

Michael once more closed his eyes and eased back into the trance. Satisfied that he could return at will, Michael once again floated free from his body. He continued floating upward until he was at the rafters of the eight foot ceiling.

Looking down at the small room, he could see his friends still in quiet conversation, while Brian continued to sit in the corner, watching Michael's empty body. Wanting to explore this new power, Michael continued floating up and out through the roof of the cabin. He received no sensations as he passed through the solid roof, nor could he feel the chill of the night air. This close to the ocean it would be cool and moist, but all Michael felt was the warmth of the fire in the cabin room.

Looking around him, Michael could see he had floated nearly one hundred feet above the forest floor. The heavily wooded land extended as far as he could see; his view cut off inland by the rugged low mountains. In the other direction he could see the ocean, startlingly close, with the moonlight glistening on the waves as they rushed to shore.

He turned to the south, their destination, and began moving toward Acantha's keep. He quickly picked up speed as he soared over the tops of the giant pine trees. The feeling of this unrestrained flight was exhilarating, and he reveled in the freedom of his spirit. He could not feel the dragging weight of his body that always tried to pull him back to earth when he floated.

If anyone had been on the forest floor, and happened to look up as Michael streaked overhead, they would have seen nothing. It was only his spirit that flew through the night.

He lowered his flight until he was below the tops of the trees, briefly dodging between them at an alarming rate of speed. He soon stopped trying to go around the trees and allowed himself to soar straight through them. Once again he felt nothing. The only sensation he had from flying through the trunks of the massive trees was the brief flickering of darkness, like the slow blinking of the eyes.

The density of the forest quickly gave way to the rich greenness of grasses and low shrubs. The darkness of the night made it difficult to see the forms of the bushes, and the contour of the ground. Suddenly he burst from the final growth of the smaller trees and found himself over gently rolling hills. He continued on, knowing that Acantha's keep would be reached in a matter of minutes at this speed. He briefly saw about a dozen forms lumbering down a hillside below him as he flashed overhead. He was past them and across the other side of the hill before he realized the forms were wrong, alien to anything he had seen before.

Instantly he stopped, once more floating above the ground as he pondered what he had seen. At a much slower rate of speed, he began to retrace his path. Crossing over the crest of the hill, he saw the same figures beginning to climb the next hillside. They were moving much more quickly than he had first thought, they were nearly out of sight already. Moving more rapidly, he chased after the retreating band. As he got closer he saw the disfigured lumbering gait of the gruesome beasts. Some were moving on all fours, some running nearly upright then falling to all fours for a few strides before thrusting themselves upright again.

Once nearly over them, Michael got his first close look. There were nearly a dozen creatures, moving rapidly, faster than a man could run at full speed. They were a dark, dirty red with occasional mottled gray areas on their hairless bodies that flaked and peeled as they ran. Their bodies were misshapen, some of the limbs sprouting from the bodies at the wrong angle, accounting for the lumbering gait.

The beasts that ran upright had long razor sharp claws on the ends of their front legs. When they dropped to run on all fours the claws did not retract, forcing them to return to an upright posture. The pain the beasts felt when trying to run on the exposed claws caused them to howl, gnashing long teeth at any of the pack that happened to come too close to them. All of them had long, sharply-pointed teeth coated in a foam-flecked bile that reflected the moon with a pale, sickly yellow light.

Reaching the edge of the woodlands, the beasts crashed through the brush with a wild abandon. Leaves, twigs, and pine needles flew in disarray and cascaded to earth in the wake of their passage. One of the beasts, too reckless in its wild, ravaging onslaught, crashed into a small pine tree in its path. Impaling itself on a broken limb, it screamed out its pain as it broke apart, spewing bile like an engorged blood blister. It hung unheeded from the limb of the tree while the rest of its brood continued its charge.

These devil's spawn could have only one origin – Acantha – and Michel knew that she was unleashing them in an attack on the cabin! With the strong need to warn and protect his friends, Michael began the trip back. The ground below him was an exploding blur as he traveled. In a matter of seconds he covered the distance necessary to return to the cabin.

With force sufficient to bowl him over, he snapped back into his body. As Michael flew across the room from the force of reentering his body, Brian let out a startled yelp. One minute he sat calmly watching, nearly asleep, and the next the magician was rolling across the floor from no force the boy could see. At the boy's exclamation, the others that were still talking by the fire jumped to their feet. Sarah was the first to reach Michael's side.

"Are you all right?" she asked worriedly, as she knelt by Michael's side.

He stirred as though coming out of a deep sleep. Groggily sitting up once again, he looked from dazed eyes at Sarah. "All right? Yes, I think so." He looked at his hands as though they were alien to him.

"What happened, Michael?" asked Everett, as he approached. Everett could clearly see that something unusual had occurred, he just did not know what. With effort, Michael pulled his gaze from his hands. He saw Everett staring at him with concern. He looked from one face to another in the small dimly lit cabin room.

"I left myself," he offered lamely.

Thomas and Oliver exchanged questioning glances with each other at Michael's attempt to offer explanation.

"What do you mean, you left yourself?" asked Everett.

Michael was finally able to explain what had happened in the last hour; from the first realization that he was free from his body, through the wondrous trip over the forest, to when he spotted the ghoulish creatures that were making the maniacal charge from the south.

"When will they be here?" asked Everett, readily willing to accept Michael's story without question.

"I don't know. Before dawn, anyway."

"What are we going to do?" asked Sarah.

"We prepare a defense," answered Thomas with a gleam in his eye. "Come on, Oliver. We've got work to do."

Three hours later, in the early pre-dawn hours, the group had made all the preparations they could and were waiting for the attack inside the small, sealed cabin.

The windows were shuttered and bolted, as was the door. A blazing fire was burning in the fireplace to provide light, and to insure against the unlikely event that one of the beasts would try to use the chimney as a means of entry. Two heavy double-bladed axes, sharpened to a razor's edge, were brought in for Thomas and Oliver. Sarah was holding an oak pitchfork; the tines brought to wicked points. Esther and Brian were huddled in a corner of the cabin; Brian bravely holding the club he had threatened the travelers with just a day earlier. Michael and Everett's hands were empty, but ready to dispense magic.

They did not have long to wait, shortly after they had locked themselves inside the cabin, the ten remaining creatures that Michael had seen miles to the south came lopping into the small clearing that sheltered the cabin.

The dark red hairless bodies were almost invisible in the dim light. Only the scarlet red eyes, reflecting the pale starlight, could readily be seen.

The unnatural beasts slowed to a stop once the cabin was in sight. It seemed as though they were deciding how best to proceed with the attack. In truth, Acantha was guiding the beasts, and was watching the attack as it unfolded, through the eyes of one of the beasts.

With a blood-chilling howl, the creatures rushed to the cabin en masse, expecting to overwhelm unsuspecting victims. The charge was aimed at the door in the center of the front wall of the cabin. They were charging up a gentle slope and did not see the hastily camouflaged pit until it was too late. The shallow pit was dug the length of the front porch area and covered with a thin layer of branches and leaves. As the first of the beasts crashed through the thin covering, it fell a scant two feet before impaling itself on sharpened posts driven into the floor of the pit. Its wild thrashing sprayed blood and bile over the floor of the porch and the other beasts as they frantically tried to correct their course or jump over the pit.

Two more of the beasts were unable to avoid the pit, as the wild jostling prevented them from altering course or jumping clear. They, too, were impaled by sharpened stakes and added their blood to the already drenched porch.

The seven remaining creatures that were able to throw themselves over the pit landed on the blood-coated floor of the porch. The slick substance on the wood planking threw them from their feet as they slid uncontrolled into the front wall of the cabin. One of the beasts struck the door headfirst, nearly knocking it from its hinges. The creature's neck was broken on impact, spilling even more blood on the floor of the porch, seeping under the door and into the cabin.

Hearing the angry howls, screams of pain, and the wild thrashing, Big Thomas and Oliver grabbed rope ends that rested on the cabin floor. The ropes were threaded through small holes that the men had gouged through the front wall of the cabin. They were attached to the bottom of the supporting beams for the porch roof. The beams had been worked loose from the flooring before the men had locked themselves in the cabin.

Thomas and Oliver pulled the ropes with all their might, ripping the support beams from the roof of the porch. The rending and crashing of the wood told the travelers that they had been successful in bringing the roof down. Two more of the beasts were caught in the collapse.

The door of the cabin burst open as one of the beams from the porch crashed against it. The four remaining beasts lunged at the opening. The first creature through the door was pulling its body using the front legs only; the two rear legs had been smashed by the falling timber and were being dragged uselessly behind.

The beast was still dangerous, viciously snapping foam-covered fangs at the people in the cabin. Oliver quickly dispatched the beast with a deadly swing of his axe.

The last three surged through the broken cabin door in a snarling, gnashing heap. The first broke directly at Thomas, who with an easy upward swing of the axe gutted the creature as it leaped for him. The second charged straight toward the back of the cabin at Michael and Everett. The pair of magicians were more than a match for the hapless beast. Bolts of fire from the pair of magicians hit the beast at the same time. The room was showered in a rain of blood as the creature literally exploded.

The remaining beast raced directly to the corner where Esther had shrunk from the violence. Her small son, Brian, was standing over her with his club raised, determined to save his mother from the nightmare that was crashing down on them. As the beast gathered itself for the final lunge at the helpless victims before it, Brian closed his eyes and swung his club with all his might, throwing his hip into the swing just like his dad had taught him when using an axe.

Yelling with fear and anger, Brian felt the recoil as the club connected on the head of the beast. His entire body was jolted and vibrated with the force of the blow. The creature howled its agony as its body was thrown off course and into the wall beside the pair. Sarah was upon it and drove the tines of the pitchfork through it before it had a chance to make an attempt at regaining its feet.

The attack had lasted only a minute but the cabin looked as though it had survived a siege of hours. The defenders looked about them in shock as the silence of the night engulfed them.

"Damn, but that was fun," chortled Thomas, with a smile on his face, as he leaned on his axe.

"Oh please, Thomas!" spat Sarah. "Not now." She slid down the wall to embrace the frightened Esther, as the men stared.

"Well, fun or not," Michael finally said, "we had better make sure we got them all."

Michael cautiously led the men out to the destruction in front of the cabin. Everett was left to protect the three still inside as Michael, Thomas, and Oliver split up to search around the outside of the cabin. Michael and Oliver had just returned when Thomas came scurrying around the corner of the cabin. "Fire! There's a fire started behind the cabin where the wood ends!"

The three men ran from the front of the cabin back in the direction that Thomas had come from. The fire was small but growing rapidly. Brush had been piled from the thick growth of bushes behind the cabin. The flames were already reaching over Michael's head, and crawling along the dried brush toward the cabin, as he raced around the corner. With hands waving in the air, Michael constructed another of his green bubbles over the area being consumed by the fire. Within minutes, without air to feed it, the fire began to die. Unnaturally quiet, with head bowed and mouth set in a tight scowl, Michael spun to return to the cabin.

"Come on," was all he said as he passed Thomas and Oliver.

Back in the cabin, Michael paced from one end of the small room to the other as Thomas and Oliver told the others about the fire. His face was set in a scowl as he continued his pacing.

"What's wrong, Michael?" Sarah asked. "You found the fire and put it out before it did any harm."

Michael stopped his pacing and looked at each member of his party in turn. The frown was still on his face when he spoke. "Yeah, I put it out. What I want to know is who started it! These beasts weren't clever enough to do it." He waved his arms toward the front of the cabin to indicate the creatures that had attacked them. "So who does that leave?"

He went on. "Dry brush was stacked against the back wall. That fire was set by human hands, and the intention was to burn down this cabin; probably hoping to kill anyone that didn't get out in time."

"But there's no one here but us," objected Everett.

"That's precisely what I mean," answered Michael.

All of the friends looked at each other, hoping not to see a guilty face.

"Oh, that's ridiculous," argued Oliver. "None of us would do that."

"There's got to be another explanation," offered Thomas.

"I don't know," Michael sighed. "We'll worry about it in the morning. For now we have enough to do. We need to clean this place up, and secure the door, so that we can get a few hours of sleep."

The members of Michael's group went about the chores of cleaning the cabin in silence, as they thought about the possibility of one of their friends working against them.

CHAPTER 20

The next morning little was said about the fire, or who might possibly have set it. Instead they began building the flying sailing vessel.

"All we really need," said Oliver by way of instruction, "is just a sled with seats on it. We'll need side rails, of course, to keep landlubbers like Thomas from falling over the side."

"Me?" responded the mountain man, wounded by the barb. "I never fall out of my seat...unless I've had too much ale, of course."

Thomas' admission helped to lighten the mood, and the travelers once again began to work together in good spirits. The men worked through the afternoon, fashioning and shaping the wood they had cut the previous night. Esther was busy inside the cabin with Sarah sewing the rough cloth she had been using as drapes for the open windows into the sails that Oliver had specified. Brian spent the afternoon helping the men with the woodwork. He practically worshiped Michael, and was in awe of the magic that he had seen the man perform.

"Do ya' think maybe I could come with ya', Michael?" he asked at the first occasion that the two were alone. "I'm a good fighter. Ya' saw me bash in that crummy beast, didn't ya'?"

"Yes, I saw," Michael answered. He stopped the work he was doing and tilted his head toward the cabin. "That's why I feel good about leaving you here. Your mother is a fine woman. She doesn't deserve to be left alone. I'm glad she has a brave young man like you to protect her."

Michael looked down at Brian and saw that the boy was staring at the cabin. "You wouldn't want her to be left alone, would you?" he asked.

"No," Brian answered slowly. "I guess I didn't think about Mom being alone. I think maybe I'd better stay here."

Michael clapped Brian on the shoulder as the two went back to the work of building the craft.

By late afternoon the flying boat was completed. It was quite simple, just flat boarding about eight feet long, with one trapezium sail supported by a yard and boom. Notches were cut along the outside of the planking where the travelers would sit. This would allow their legs to drop over either side, as though they were riding bareback. A railing was built along both sides for safety.

"Well, what do you think?" asked Oliver when Everett walked over to join him alongside the flying boat.

"Not much to look at," replied Everett, somberly.

"It doesn't need to be pretty, Everett...just functional. We don't need to cut through waves, or keep from being swamped by taking on water, so all we need is what you see here."

Michael and Thomas joined the pair as they stood examining the new craft.

"Not very pretty," remarked Big Thomas.

"Yeah, doesn't look like much," agreed Michael.

"Aahhh!" wailed Oliver, as he threw his hands in the air and stalked to the cabin. "Functional! Functional!" he shouted as he marched to the cabin without looking back.

"What's gotten into him?" inquired Michael of Everett.

"I'm not sure," mused Everett. "I think he wants everyone to see this thing as pretty."

"Why would he want that? All that matters is that it works."

Everett shrugged his shoulders as the three men began the walk back to the cabin.

They decided to make the first attempt at flying Oliver's air-boat after a late lunch. Of course everyone showed for the first attempt. Oliver would be piloting, with Michael on board to do his magic and keep the boat flying.

"Okay," said Oliver, "now, I'll keep the sail filled, you keep the craft in the air."

"I don't see any problem with that," answered Michael.

"Yeah, but you gotta do more than that," continued Oliver. "The wind is blowing in from the west; if we want to go south, that means you gotta keep pressure on the port side of the craft so that we don't get pushed east."

Michael looked at Oliver as though he were suddenly speaking a foreign language.

"I don't understand a word you said, Oliver."

"No, I don't suppose you do," sighed Oliver, as he put his hands on his hips. "Let me see if I can explain this so that even a landlubber like you can understand. Okay, it's like this." Oliver pointed toward the ocean. "The wind is coming in from the west, but we want to go south." Oliver pointed to the south. "The wind will be pushing us from the right side, not from behind, that means we'll be pushed to the left. But we don't want to go left...understand?"

"Sure, I've got you so far."

"Good. So, if you keep pressure on the left side of the craft, we won't be able to go in that direction, and the wind will sort of 'squirt' us straight ahead. If we were sailing in the ocean, the water on the hull of the boat would act as that pressure, but since we don't have any water, we use your magic instead."

"Right, I think I've got it. Besides, I'm sure you'll quickly tell me if I'm not doing what you expect."

"You'll do fine. Get on behind me, I need to be in the bow to handle these lines."

Michael and Oliver sat on the length of planking making up the hull of the air-boat. The sail was down as Michael began raising the boat. When they had reached the top of the tree line, Oliver pulled one of the ropes he was holding, and the sail began to travel up the mast.

As the sail filled with air, the vessel surged sideways. "Pressure on the left, Michael. Pressure on the left. Don't let us drift sideways."

As Michael used his magic to stop the air-boat from moving to the left, he found it beginning to tip over on the left side.

"Push down on the right side!" yelled Oliver, as he grabbed the railing to keep from being pitched over the side.

Michael fought to keep the craft level, as Oliver finally regained his balance and began to maneuver the sail. Once righted and the sail filled again, the vessel surged ahead. A few tense seconds passed when Michael and Oliver were flipped on their side, but when they had corrected and began actually sailing south the group left on the ground celebrated with cheers and handshaking. Brian was jumping up and down, clapping, and cheering all at the same time. His head was craned back in an almost impossible position to watch the two men overhead.

Michael and Oliver were now flying over the tops of the trees at an amazing rate of speed. Oliver had never sailed such a fast vessel before.

"This is wonderful, Michael!" he called over his shoulder. "There's no friction from the water to slow us down. We're literally flying with the wind!"

"Great! Let's turn it around and head back. We'll try it with everyone on board."

Their robes flapped in the air, and their hair swirled around their heads as Oliver used the wind to turn the air-boat back the way they had come. Michael reversed the instructions Oliver had given him earlier, and they were soon back to where their flight had originated. Oliver untied one of the ropes and lowered the sail as they approached the clearing where their friends waited for them. As they drifted into the clearing, Michael lowered the air-boat slowly to the ground. They were greeted by handshakes and backslaps when they finally landed.

"Marvelous, simply marvelous contraption, Oliver," said Everett, as he pumped his hands in congratulations.

"Never doubted you, ya' old coot!" boomed a smiling Thomas.

"Hey. What about me!" objected Michael.

"You were wonderful, too, Michael," said Sarah, hugging him tenderly. "But, why did you almost tip the boat over when Oliver put up the sail?"

"Oh brother! Such respect we magicians get. Come on. We're going to take a test flight with everyone on board."

There was a strong sense of excitement as Sarah, Thomas, and Everett clambered on board. Sarah was seated directly behind Michael, with Big Thomas behind her. Everett was on the back end of the craft; he was to levitate anyone that might get tossed overboard.

Esther and Brian stood to the side and watched as the group prepared for the second test flight. Michael saw the longing in Brian's eyes as he watched his new friends.

"Come on along, Brian," Michael said. "It's time to have a little bit of fun."

Brian's elation quickly turned to disappointment when his mother started to protest.

"It will be okay, Esther," Michael quickly assured her. "If he begins to fall, Everett will keep him above ground until we can return for him. Just as easy as this." With a wave of Michael's hand, Brian's feet left the ground, and he was floating six feet in the air, the boy's legs thrashing, and arms pin wheeling to keep his balance. But the squeals of delight showed that he was not frightened by the new experience. With additional assurances from Everett, Esther finally agreed to allow her son to join them on their flight.

It was hard to tell who was the most excited when the air-boat rose from the ground, Brian or Sarah. She was thrilled by the new experience of flying. It was exhilarating to travel over the rugged terrain, without the dragging effects of physical exertion. She was aware of every sensation during the short trip...the hard rough planking that threatened to shoot rough slivers into her soft flesh, the freedom of her legs that were dangling from the side of the craft. The wind above the sheltered woodlands cooled her, even as she threw her head back to feel the warmth of the late afternoon sun on her face.

"Why didn't anyone think of this before now, Michael?" she asked.

"I suppose all of the magicians were too busy trying to go about their business unnoticed. How long would they have remained unnoticed, flying through the heavens on pieces of wood?"

As Sarah watched the beauty of the surrounding countryside slip past her, she became aware of Brian's hands anchored in the folds of the back of the jacket that she wore. He was sitting on Big Thomas' lap, holding onto Sarah, just in front of him.

"What do you think about all of this, Brian?" she asked.

"It's great!" he exclaimed. "Anyone that can make this happen, is sure to be able to rescue my dad."

No answer was necessary; either they would be successful or they wouldn't. There was no sense in giving the boy doubt.

The test lasted about an hour with Oliver and Michael practicing turning maneuvers, and sailing different directions. When they returned, it was near dusk; Esther had a fire going, preparing dinner.

They would stay one more night before returning to their travels.

CHAPTER 21

Early the next morning, Michael and Everett went off by themselves for a walk by the stream, while the others prepared the air-boat for travel. Thomas and Oliver were busy loading their supplies, while Sarah helped Esther put the finishing touches on cleaning the cabin. Against his vocal wishes, Brian was left behind.

"So, what's on your mind that you pulled me away from everyone else?" Everett inquired.

"That fire, Everett," Michael replied as he sat on an embankment overlooking the small stream. "One of us started it."

Everett sat beside Michael, and sighed as he began gently tossing pebbles into the stream. "I've been thinking about that ever since we were so unceremoniously ejected from the Church of the Second Millennium. One of our people told them that we were magicians."

Michael looked over at his old friend and nodded his head to indicate that he had been thinking the same thing. "It's too much to believe that Acantha could have positioned a spy in the right place months ago. Could she have reached one of us over this kind of distance, and coerced them to do her will?"

"I'm sure that she could," replied Everett. "And whoever that person is, I don't believe they even know what they are doing.

"It could be any one of them...or us," Everett continued as he looked over at the young magician.

Michael shook his head to answer Everett's thought that the problem could be with one of the magicians.

"No, not you or me. I don't think she could get that kind of control over me anymore. If she can, we're in big trouble. And I don't think it could be you. You were inside the cabin with Sarah when the fire broke out. That leaves Big Thomas or Oliver."

Everett leaned back until he was lying on the small grassy hillock. He stared up at the clear spring sky as he spoke to Michael. "I'm getting too old for this, son. I should be reclining in an old wooden rocking chair somewhere rather than traipsing across the countryside, battling evil magic. We need to make an end of this."

Everett sat back up and looked over at Michael with a concerned look on his face. "Are you ready, Michael? Can you better Acantha's power?"

Everett had put words to the fears that Michael had felt. His power was growing steadily every day, but Acantha had been using her powers longer than he had. There would be no second chance. If he failed in defeating Acantha and the strength of the ruby, he would become just another fatality, joining all of the lost friends from the magician's enclave.

He stood and turned his face from the old master to hide the doubt that he knew was reflected there. "I don't know, Everett, but it's too late to worry about that now. With Oliver's flying air-boat, we'll be at the keep in a matter of days, rather than the weeks it would have taken us before."

Everett stood to join his friend, but tactfully let him continue to face away. "Well...I guess we'll worry about it when we get there. For now we have to figure out who among us is helping her – unwittingly or otherwise. Come, it is time to take up our journey again."

When Michael and Everett returned to the cabin, everyone was outside by the new air-boat. Thomas and Oliver were lashing the supplies to the side of the vessel, while Sarah stood saying good-bye to Esther and Brian. Her arm was around Brian's shoulders, and he was looking up at the beautiful young woman with adoring eyes.

"Oh, there you two are," she said as they approached. "Are we ready to go?"

"I guess we are," answered Michael. "Let's just see how Thomas and Oliver are getting along with the supplies."

They all walked over to where the two men were putting the finishing touches on preparing the vessel. The innovative air-boat sat in the clearing looking like a child's randomly assembled toy. Thomas was securing the last of the supplies, while Oliver looked on.

"How goes it, Thomas?" asked Michael as the approached.

"Good," Thomas answered. "Our hosts gave us a couple of gifts." He pointed at the two double bladed axes that were tied to the side of the vessel.

"That's a good idea," Everett responded. "I'm afraid we may need them. Acantha may have more of those beasts lined up for us."

"We've even got that pitch-fork that Sarah used," added Thomas.

"I would give you anything I have, if it would help you to free my husband," said Esther as she lowered her head to hide the tears that were forming in her eyes.

Everett took one of her hands in his, patting it to comfort her. "My dear child, we will do our very best to help free your husband and his brother. I wish we could promise you that we will succeed, but..."

"I know you will do all you can," replied Esther as her teary eyes began to smile. "Come back and see us when you are through. My husband and I will give you a feast you'll not soon forget."

"Marvelous idea!" boomed Thomas. "We'll be successful, if for no other reason than that."

The travelers all took their seats on the air-boat, and prepared for Michael to lift it off the ground, when Brian approached. "Ya' going to bring my dad back?" he asked Michael.

"We're going to try."

The young boy thought for a minute before he continued. "I'm going to learn how to respect magic, like ya' said, then I'm going to be a magician, just like you."

"If you put your mind to it, Brian, I'm sure you will."

Esther and Brian stood back and waved as the flying air-boat lifted from the ground, slowly gaining altitude until it was above the top of the trees. Oliver once again raised sail and allowed the wind to fill it. Michael, alert to what to expect this time, managed to keep the vessel level as the wind sent it on its way.

The rough conditions of the previous few weeks were quickly forgotten as the five sailed over the lush green beauty of the coastal forest. It went unsaid, but all of the members knew the conflict was now near at hand. If they had continued their travels by foot, it would have taken them another month to beat a path through the dense undergrowth to Acantha's keep. With the air-boat that Oliver had envisioned and they had built, they would be there in just a couple of days.

As they slipped quietly over the tops of the trees, Sarah leaned forward and rested her head on the back of Michael's shoulder. "It's beautiful up here, Michael. You can see everything, the green hills, rocky beaches, the sun shining on the ocean."

"I can understand how unusual this is to you," he responded. "I remember how it felt the first time I floated more than just a couple of feet off the ground."

"Did you ever get tired of it? I mean, all of this beauty, how could you get tired of it."

"No," answered Michael with a chuckle. "I suppose I got use to floating above the trees, but I never got tired of the feeling of freedom."

Big Thomas looked over the top of Sarah's head, to Michael. "How high could we go, Michael? I mean, is this the limit -- or how much higher could we go?"

"What's the matter, Thomas?" Oliver called back. "Isn't a couple of hundred feet of the ground high enough for you?"

"Sure it is," he responded. "Until we come upon a mountain that's a couple of hundred feet higher than us, that is."

"I honestly can't tell you how high we could go, Thomas," replied Michael. "I'd rather not take any chances. This is something all of us are unfamiliar with."

"Boy, what a view though," Thomas continued. "Isn't this just the prettiest thing you ever saw, Sarah?"

Sarah looked over her shoulder, and the wind gently ruffled her hair until it covered her face. "It sure is," Sarah answered as she tried in vain to push her hair from her face. "I'd like to come over the hills into Monterey flying like this. I'll bet that's even prettier."

They sailed on for another two hours before Michael became tired and asked Everett to use his magic to support the air-boat. Everett's efforts lasted less than an hour before he needed to lower the air-boat to the ground so they could all rest.

"I'm not complaining, you know," said Sarah when she climbed off the now grounded air-boat. "But, I wish we had thought to put some cloth on the boards where we sit." She noticed she was not the only one that was gently massaging their backsides.

"Yeah, I think I'm going to have to agree with you," replied Everett.

"Just a bunch of soft landlubbers," taunted Oliver. "Look, we just made as much progress in a couple of hours that would have taken us days if we were still walking. With a bit of rest, we can sail for another couple of hours."

Understanding how quickly they were traveling brought back to everyone how soon it would be that they would confront Acantha. None of them knew if they had the strength, or if Michael had the power to survive, let alone win the battle. After a couple of minutes, it was Sarah who broke the fumbling silence. "Well, if you men want to eat before we start off again, we had better get to work. We need a fire and some of the supplies brought from the air-boat."

While the other men were unloading what Sarah had specified that she needed for making lunch, she stole off for a few minutes alone with Michael.

"You know," she began, "a few days ago I would have tried to convince you to put this fool's errand behind you. I still felt that perhaps you could turn away from it, and we could go back to normal lives. Now, after the attack on the cabin, and knowing that Brian's father was stolen away, I see what Everett meant when he said that Acantha would never let you live in peace."

"Sarah, I know it's not fair to you..."

"That's not my point, Michael," she interrupted. She stopped and put one hand on Michael's shoulder and looked up at him. "My point is, I understand now that this woman -- no matter that she's your sister – needs to be stopped. I also understand that you may be the only one capable of stopping her."

"I have to try," said Michael, returning Sarah's gaze.

"I know you do. I just wanted you to know that I agree with you; and I'll be with you all the way."

Michael smiled as he pulled her into his arms. "How did I get so lucky, to find you?"

"And don't you forget it," she replied playfully. "Come on, we had better get back to the others before they think we are getting overly romantic."

He caught her arm as she pulled away. "Not a bad idea, you know. We haven't had that much time to ourselves lately."

"Michael...what if one of the others comes looking for us?"

"Don't worry. No one will see a thing." Michael punctuated his promise by raising his right arm and circling it around their heads. "Now, if anyone comes looking for us, they'll pass right by."

Sarah sighed deeply as she once again moved into his embrace.

*     *     *     *     *

Acantha cursed and slammed her fist against the table, as the two forms in her magical bowl disappeared from sight. "So easy...it's getting so damned easy for him."

She spun around to face the shadowy figure behind her. It was the forlorn, shattered man that Sarah had first seen crashing through her doorway weeks earlier.

"If you had done as I instructed in the first place," shrieked Acantha, as she pointed a wickedly accusing finger at him, "I wouldn't be faced with them approaching my very door."

Croom made a futile gesture with one hand and continued staring at the floor in front of Acantha.

"I did what I could. His magic was stronger than yours."

Acantha spent nearly thirty seconds sputtering in an uncontrolled rage. "His power is not stronger than mine!" she finally shouted.

"I merely meant, the distance was so great. He was immediately in front of me, and you were so very far away." Croom raised his eyes without raising his head to see if his words were soothing her rage. Her face, however, was still a vivid red from his unintentional barb.

Although Croom was already dead, there were greater things than death that she could -- in fact already had -- threatened him with. Fearing an eternal state of limbo between death and life, Croom tried once again to soothe the irate sorceress.

"You nearly defeated him at the church, and again on the cliffs with the avalanche. It was only by blind luck that he escaped."

She finally calmed her rage, as she stalked across the stone floor of her laboratory. She stopped in front of the wretched dead man. "For once you are speaking as though your brain has not rotted completely away."

She moved to a comfortably padded chair and sat. Taking a flute of wine from the table beside the chair, she daintily sipped while thinking what her next move should be. "I have mended that putrefying hole in your chest. Do you think perhaps you could approach Michael and his cronies without alerting every animal within a mile's radius this time?"

She regarded Croom over the rim of her glass as she spoke. Knowing how utterly in her power he was, she gave a wicked smile waiting for his answer.

Croom lifted his head. Now, rather than the floor, he was staring at the ceiling. "Whatever it takes, Acantha. You caused my death, and you caused my rebirth. All I want is to return to oblivion. I would take one hundred people with me, if that was what was needed to gain my release."

Acantha threw her head back and laughed loudly. "Oh, Croom. You are such a humanitarian." She raised her glass to him. "I should propose a toast to you." Lowering her glass, she added, "But, I think perhaps I'll wait and see if you can do better this time.

"Now leave me," she said as she stood once more. "I'll call you when I'm ready."

Croom slowly backed out of the door of Acantha's laboratory, never taking his eyes off the sorceress. If it had been in his power he would have taken her with him back into the abyss of death.

Knowing his thoughts, Acantha's smile turned even more malicious. "Yes, Croom," she whispered to herself. "Harbor that hatred in your heart. It may serve you well when I call upon you."

CHAPTER 22

Michael and his friends had finally passed the southern edge of the great forest they had been traveling above. Later in the afternoon they made camp on one of the sandy coves.

There were still a few hours of sunlight left, and Thomas and Oliver were trying their luck at fishing for some of the smaller fish that frequented the surf. Oliver had brought plenty of line, and a few of the precious fish-hooks that he had made from what pieces of metal that he could find around the village of Monterey that weren't rusted.

The bait that they used was plentiful. As the waves rolled out the men would simply dig into the wet sand, pulling out burrowing sand crabs. Oliver showed his greater knowledge of the art of fishing by doubling Thomas' catch. The evening meal consisted of filets of ocean perch, mostly provided by Oliver.

It was still early when they were finished with dinner. Michael once again separated himself from the main group to meditate. While Sarah and the others passed the time in idle conversation, Michael easily slipped back into a trance. Everett watched out of the corner of one eye while the young magician explored the mysteries of his growing powers.

Michael sat quietly in meditation for over an hour, learning more about his potential than he thought was possible. After that, he opened the eyes in his mind, while the eyes of his body were still closed. He saw his friends sitting on the beach around the campfire. Like he did at the cabin in the woods, he once again left his body. Without fear this time, he felt his spirit soar as it was released from the earthly confines forced upon him. He saw that the sun was just beginning to set, firing the ocean view in a brilliant orange glow.

His friends were quiet now, watching the setting sun, or lost in their private thoughts. Michael could see that Everett was watching the body that the young magician had just left. The old master was very interested in Michael's progress. Michael could understand this, since the entire group's survival depended on his being able to control the magic of the emerald.

Once again Michael began the exhilarating trip south, spirit flying free. They were much closer to their goal now, and it took Michael but moments to travel to Acantha's keep. He was nearly overcome with remembered grief as he saw what had at one time been the only home he had known. Michael and Acantha had grown up in the magician's enclave. They had learned the rudiments of magic together. They had laughed and played together.

That was over now. This place of memories had become a killing ground. Beside his family, Michael had lost countless friends in one short afternoon. Acantha was lost to him as well. Though she still lived, she was no longer his beloved sister.

He remembered that terrible day as his spirit, or consciousness, soared over the green hillside leading up to the keep. As he approached, he saw the delicate fairyland appearance from a distance, and thought of its true massive strength when seen closely. Strength and beauty vied equally throughout. Lush gardens watched over by exquisite marble statues outdoors, and mixtures of rough stonework and massive dark wood enclosing antique furnishings and delicate artwork inside.

The sun had nearly set and the beautiful castle was now shrouded in shadow. The towers stood out like stone monoliths against the rapidly darkening sky. Michael slowed his approach as he reached the grounds of the massive building. The gardens, that had once been tended so lovingly, had begun to degenerate into a weed-choked remnant of their former glory. He tried to turn his attention to finding Acantha, in hopes that if he did not notice the deterioration, it would make it less tragic.

He smoothly melted into and through the wall of the building. Inside was a large darkened room. An ornate oak dining table with chairs to match dominated the room. On the walls were beautiful paintings from antiquity. A fine layer of undisturbed dust covered everything in the room, indicating its lack of use.

Seeing the room in such a lonely state brought fresh feelings of remorse to Michael. This was the dining room used by the elders of the magician's enclave. The younger apprentices, from age ten to fifteen, would serve the elders their meals in this room, taking their own dinners in the kitchen after the elders had finished. Every young apprentice went through this period of service, as a means to learn respect for their elders, and humility for themselves.

He remembered vividly some of the occasions when he and Acantha performed this service. He remembered feeling honored to serve the master magicians. His parent's smiles of pride were still fresh in his mind. It grieved him to see this magnificent room left to die as his friends had died. Not wishing to see more, he continued his hunt for Acantha. He instinctively headed for the uppermost portions of the keep. He traveled through deserted hallways, and more neglected rooms. The first tower he reached was empty, and had been for many months. Reaching into the other areas of the keep with his power alone, he detected the strong emanation of magic coming from one of the other towers.

Michael slowly left the tower he was in. By traveling through the wall and over the roof of the keep, he reached and entered the tower where he had sensed the strength of magic. He entered this time into Acantha's laboratory. In direct contrast to the other portions of the keep that he had just left, this room was obviously in constant use. The worktable was cluttered with materials used in the performance of magic; materials both normal and arcane. In the middle of the clutter was a beautiful cut-crystal bowl. It was empty and gleamed from a recent cleaning. Acantha's evil powers clung to it like a funeral shroud.

Aside from the clutter, the room was empty. Michael left it and entered the marble and stone hallway. At one end of the hall were two men with mops and wooden buckets.

"I haven't seen that wicked bitch all day," said one of the men.

"Sshh! Watch your tone." replied the other. "I wouldn't put it past her to be able to hear you."

"Yeah, well what's it matter? How long are we going to put up with this?"

Rather than answering right away, the second man went back to mopping the floor furiously. He spent the next thirty seconds or so trying to ignore the pointed stare of the first.

"Look," he finally said as he stopped his work and leaned on the mop. "I don't know what kind of mess we've gotten into here, and I don't think we can do anything about it until we know more. Every time we beat feet for the door, that decayed ghoul is there waiting for us."

"You aren't suggesting that we accept what's happened to us, are you?"

"No, I'm saying we should know what we're doing before we do it."

Michael moved closer to the two men as they were talking. Listening to them, he came to the conclusion that these were the men that Acantha had taken from Esther and Brian. The man that had been declaring a need for caution rather than recklessness, showed a remarkable resemblance to Brian. The two men looked as though they were brothers.

"Can you hear me?" inquired Michael as he hovered above the two men. They continued their conversation with no indication that they were aware of his presence.

He lowered until he was directly between them. "Hear me!" he demanded.

Michael gave an emotional sigh as the men went back to work. He traveled back down the hall the way he had come. He figured that Acantha would stay in a small portion of the keep, and would be near the laboratory.

After searching just a short time he found her. She was in one of the larger rooms on the floor directly beneath her laboratory. She had converted it into a bedroom, it was filled with lace and chintz. Against the far wall was a massive canopied bed. Acantha was not alone. Sweat-flecked and straining, a repugnant fat man was seated on the floor taking great joy in cleaning all of Acantha's shoes. The fat man, rather than acting like a captive, was giggling and chortling with pleasure.

Michael was shamed to see his once-beloved sister enjoying the dominance of the man. As he was watching the man, Acantha sensed his presence. Before he could leave, she whipped her head in all directions, trying to see the presence that she had sensed. She was angry and scowling when she realized there was no one in the room.

"Stop!" she demanded.

"What?" whined Milo.

"Shut-up you fool. I wasn't speaking to you."

Milo lifted his head from the work, casting nervous glances around the room, looking for the intruder that Acantha was speaking to.

"There's no one else..."

She cut short what Milo was about to say with an icy glare.

"I know you're here, brother, I can feel it. Show yourself, if you're brave enough."

Michael's fear of Acantha's power, and what he remembered of the killings that happened a year ago, warred with his sense of duty. If he ran now, he would never be able to confront her.

He moved further into the room. "I am here, sister. Can you hear me?"

"Of course I can hear you! What is this, some cheap parlor trick?" She continued looking around the room, completely aware there was nowhere for Michael to hide, but unwilling to accept the fact that his powers had grown to such an extent that he could converse over a great distance.

Milo divided his time by looking around the room for the person that Acantha was talking to, and looking at her as though she had lost all sanity. He could hear no voice, other than hers.

"Who are you talking to, my dear?" he asked meekly.

"Where are you?" she demanded, ignoring Milo. "Come out here where I can see you. How did you get here so fast? That stupid air-boat of yours doesn't move that fast."

"No, you're right, it doesn't. I am still miles north of you. But my soul, or spirit, is here, I can see and hear you."

Acantha was nearly turning in circles now, trying to find something solid to fix her attention on.

"Enough of this! I saw you myself this morning. I saw you in my crystal bowl. You were still at those stupid people's shack. How are you able to do this trick of yours?"

"Do you forget, Acantha? I have the other ring. I believe it will prove to be just as powerful as yours, if not more so. In fact, I believe you did something very much like this – weeks earlier."

Giving up on finding something of substance to vent her anger on, Acantha affected nonchalance as she strode over to a chair by the window. Full night had fallen, and the open window allowed the cooling night breeze into the room.

"I don't have the faintest idea what you're talking about," she replied after taking a seat in the chair.

"I think you know exactly what I mean," Michael answered as he moved closer to where Acantha sat in mock innocence. "Sometime in the last two weeks you visited one of my friends, much in the same manner that I am using now. You put a spell on him to work against us."

"Oh, Michael...so what? Did you think that if you came to me and said, 'Pretty please' that I would leave you alone?" Acantha crossed her legs and casually rested her arms on the side of the chair. "But, I will make a deal with you. Bring me the emerald and I will release the spell on that old fisherman, and allow you all to go your own way. If not..."

"Fisherman? So it was Oliver?"

"You didn't know? Well, no matter," she said with a wave of her hand, "he wasn't a very effective ally. He did give me a laugh or two," she added, thinking of when she had surprised the old seaman in the woods.

Michael once again felt the stabbing pain of loss. How could all of this have happened? "Acantha, can't you fight this evil power that has a hold over you? Can't you see what you have become?"

"What I have become, brother," she raged in response, "is the strongest magician in the world!" She surged to her feet and furiously began to pace the floor, agitated at Michael's words.

Michael was in her path as she paced, causing Acantha to pass through him as he floated. He was shocked at the deep coldness that he felt as they passed.

"What you have become, sister, is the most dangerous magician in the world."

Stopping, Acantha raised an arrogant chin. "Enough! Agree with my terms or leave me. I have grown tired of your childish debate."

Milo was still watching Acantha carefully, and saw her relax after making the last demand. "He's gone," she said as she lowered her head in thought. "How in the hell did he gain so much power in such a short time?"

"Who were you talking to, my dear?" whispered Milo.

"I need to see them again," continued Acantha, ignoring Milo's pleas.

"My bowl!" she shouted. "Get me slaves. I need to make sure they're still miles from here."

"What about me?" whined Milo.

"You? Yes, you will do fine. You probably have lots to spare."

"No! That's not what I meant, I meant let me go and I'll find the slaves for you.

"I don't have time for that. I'll have to make do with you."

The two new slaves that Michael recognized as the men from Esther and Brian's family, heard Milo shouting one floor away. As he was being dragged up the stairs by Acantha's magic, they wisely found another section of the castle to work in.

Michael made the trip back to his body slowly, barely noticing the star-filled sky, or the surf pounding into shore as he traveled north once again. He had not imagined that he would so easily find Acantha's unwilling slave. Oliver obviously was not to blame. He was entirely unaware of whatever actions he took against his friends.

Michael would need to be careful how he solved the problem. Oliver had been valuable to the group. No one needed to know about Acantha's spell...as long as the spell could be broken.

He finally arrived back at the beach where they had made camp for the night. He easily slid back into his body and opened his eyes. Everett was lying on his side, head propped up with his arm. He was the only one awake. Michael had been meditating for two hours.

"I was beginning to worry about you," the old magician said as he sat up.

"You don't look worried," replied Michael.

Everett smiled at his young friend. "Well, I guess I have a lot of confidence in you now. Did you leave your body again?"

"Yes, I visited Acantha."

"Really? Did she know you were there?"

Michael stood to stretch muscles that had grown stiff from two hours of sitting without moving. "Yes, it's funny. I saw the two men that were kidnapped from Esther's cabin. When I tried to talk to them, they didn't respond. They didn't even know I was there. But Acantha picked up on my presence as soon as I entered her room. We had no problem communicating."

"I'm not really surprised. But tell me what happened. What did she say?"

The two talked into the night about Michael's visit to Acantha's keep. Time enough later for rest, what was needed now was information. Any information that would help them get into the keep, and wrest the ruby from Acantha.

CHAPTER 23

Michael spent the next morning deep in thought. The use of the emerald had become easy enough that he needed only slight concentration to keep the air-boat afloat. The rest of his mind was occupied with the problem of releasing Oliver from Acantha's spell. Hopefully without everyone else knowing what was happening.

"What's the problem, Michael?" Oliver asked as he tended to the sail. "You've been real quiet."

"Oh, sorry, Oliver. I've been trying to figure out how to get all of us into Acantha's keep...and then what to do once we get in."

"As strong as you've become, I don't see where we'll have any problems," the old fisherman answered.

"Right, no problems," said Michael. His thoughts were once more on the very real problem of Oliver.

They were still flying deep into the afternoon. They had stopped only once, for lunch. Michael was determined to reach the old magician's enclave before nightfall.

"It's beginning to look a lot like home, Michael," said Everett from the rear of the air-boat.

"Yeah, we're going to make it today."

"Can you see the keep yet?" asked Sarah.

"Not yet," Michael answered. "It's still a couple of hills away. It will be on the top of one of those hills over there." Michael pointed to a line of hills about five miles inland that was running parallel to the shoreline.

"There!" called out Thomas a few minutes later. "I see it. On top of that hill over there."

"That's it," agreed Everett. "Let's get this contraption on the ground, so that we can discuss our plans for getting into the castle."

"What plans?" Oliver asked. "We don't have any plans."

"I do." responded Everett. "Just land this thing, and trust me."

"I trust you, Everett," said Michael, "but, not Acantha. I'm going to put a cloaking spell around us before we land. I don't want to take a chance that she could track us to our camp."

After Michael lowered the air-boat to the ground, they unloaded the supplies from the vessel. The first items to be unloaded were the two double-bladed axes, and pitchfork given to them by Esther. Being this close to Acantha's keep gave them a fearful feeling of unease.

As they sat down to a cold meal, without a campfire, Everett began to tell them of his plans to get into the castle.

"Let's not talk about that just yet," interrupted Michael.

"Why not?" asked Everett, as he looked up at Michael in surprise. "These are things we need to talk about."

"Time enough later," answered Michael shortly.

The rest of the group looked at Michael without understanding why he would delay talking about the plan to enter the old castle, now that they were at the threshold. However, after seeing how he could keep Oliver's air-boat suspended all day, they respected the great gains he had made in controlling the emerald's power. They felt that somehow in the last few days, Michael had become the leader of the quest, rather than Everett. Because of this, they did not question his decision not to talk of their plans.

"Oliver, there are some things I must do to prepare for my battle with Acantha. Will you help me?"

"Well, of course, Michael. What do you need?"

By way of answering, Michael stood and nodded his head to the side, indicating that Oliver should follow him.

"I'll keep the cloaking spell on the campsite, and keep us cloaked as far as possible. We should be safe as long as none of you leave the area of the camp."

As Michael and Oliver left the camp, Michael extended the cloak of invisibility to include them as they walked. They had walked nearly a half of a mile before Michael felt his control of the spell weakening. He would either have to uncover the campsite or himself and Oliver.

"Where in the world are we going Michael? Why won't you tell me?"

"We're almost there, Oliver. Just a little farther."

*     *     *     *     *

Inside the castle, Acantha had been keeping an all-day vigil over her crystal bowl.

"Where did they go? Damn him and his cloaking spell!"

Milo sat on the floor, resting against the wall. He was pale-skinned, and his face was slack from the blood that Acantha had pulled from him recently. He tried to look up at Acantha when she spoke, but he lacked the energy to raise his head.

"I saw them as they approached, so they must be nearby." She continued to stare into the blood-filled crystal bowl, ignoring the whimpers that came from her discarded slave against the wall.

As she watched, Michael and Oliver finally moved past the area of influence of his cloaking spell. An evil, tooth-filled grin came over Acantha as she saw the two appear.

"I think this is far enough, Oliver."

"Far enough for what?" asked Oliver.

Now that Michael had Oliver alone, he was unsure of how to break the spell that Acantha had placed on him. He would need to be careful, he did not want to put Oliver at risk if he didn't have to. Now with Acantha's keep in sight, Michael was approaching the first true test of his powers against hers.

Michael gestured to the ground and suggested they sit in comfort.

Oliver's eyebrows lowered to hood his eyes, his lips parted showing teeth in an evil grin. "No, I'll stand." The malicious look that had come over Oliver was gone as quickly as it came. He gave no indication that he was aware of any change.

Michael was aware now that Acantha was with him, through Oliver. "Somewhere along the trip, Acantha visited one of us. She used her magic to enslave that person, and used him to work against us."

"One of us?" asked Oliver, eyes wide in surprise. Quickly his brows knit again, and a thick voice came from his suddenly sneering lips, "I wonder who that could be."

"Oliver?" Michael spoke his name to get back in touch with the friend he knew, rather that the slave that was controlled by Acantha.

"Yes, I heard you," he replied. "So who is it, and what are we going to do about it?"

Michael paused only a second before replying, "It's you, Oliver. And we're going to try to break the spell."

"Me!" Oliver exclaimed. "Nonsense! I've done no such thing."

The sneer came back to Oliver's face. "He doesn't believe you. Now what are you going to do?" Once again the sneer left his face as quickly as it came.

"Oliver, it's not your fault. You weren't even aware of it when you would do her bidding."

As Michael was speaking, Oliver reached behind his back. When he brought his hand back into view, he was holding a razor-sharp hunting knife. The wicked blade was fully eight inches long

Michael stepped back when he saw the blade. The setting sun reflected brightly off the shiny, deadly surface.

"Fight it! You've got to try to fight off the control that Acantha has over you, Oliver."

"What's happening, Michael?" asked Oliver. There was a quiver in his voice brought on by fear, and the realization of what he was doing. Oliver looked down at his hand holding the weapon as though it was totally apart from him. It was like watching the actions of a totally separate person. Actions that were completely out of Oliver's control.

"What the hell's happening, Michael?" wailed Oliver as he began stalking toward Michael.

Michael did not waste time on words. Seeing Oliver's advance he quickly enveloped himself in a hazy green light. It immediately coalesced into the vibrant bubble that he had used in the past.

Oliver's advance did not slow at the sight of Michael's shield, however the knife in his hand began to glow with a light of its own. Soon the knife and the hand holding it were encased in a vibrant red light.

Oliver stared at his hand that held the knife as it began to glow scarlet red. He looked up at Michael with pleading eyes. "Michael, help me! Don't let me do this!"

Suddenly, although his eyes pleaded not to do this thing, Oliver lunged at Michael with the knife. Michael backed away by reflex, even though protected by his shield. The knife in Oliver's hand sang through the air in an arc toward Michael. The scarlet covering connected with the emerald shield, parting it like torn paper. Both men stopped in surprise as Michael's magical shield continued to tear, edges flapping in the wind. Like a worn and discarded sheet, the fabric of the shield tore and was carried away by the early evening breeze.

Just as Oliver was gathering himself for another attack, Michael leaped into the air, making his magic lift him higher and higher off the ground. He was soon floating fifty feet off the ground.

Oliver stood below him, craning his neck to see Michael above him.

"That was a terribly foolish thing to do, Michael," came Acantha's voice from Oliver. "This is precisely why Everett didn't float above the ground when Croom was chasing you so many months ago. It seems you could still learn from the old man. All I have to do is place Oliver directly below you and float him up. If you try to descend, he's got you; if you stay where you are, he's got you. Even if you try to go higher, he'll eventually catch up with you."

Michael watched in alarm as the scarlet light enveloping Oliver's hand and knife grew to cover all of him. When he was completely covered with the malignant light, Oliver slowly began to rise from the ground, on a direct line with Michael.

Oliver was calling out to Michael in panic, "Stop me, Michael! Don't let this happen!" He continued floating up with the knife held over his head. Michael began moving higher as he watched Oliver.

Looking for inner guidance, Michael quickly lapsed into a light trance. Searching through his subconscious for the new magic provided by the emerald, he found what he hoped would be the one possibility to save himself, and release Oliver from Acantha's hold.

Unlike the other times that he had left his body, this time he left blind. There was no sight to guide him, no senses to steer him along the correct path. Rather than his soul or spirit making this short journey, it was only his intelligence, his power.

Without knowing how, Michael felt himself slip into Oliver being, felt the strangle-hold that Acantha held on him. Guided by the power of the emerald, he found that place inside Oliver that Acantha had fastened onto. He went to that spot and focused all of his power at the small tendril of evil magic that grasped Oliver's will.

With a vibration that Michael could almost feel, the hold on Oliver was broken. Michael was pulled out of his trance by Acantha's wail when her hold was broken. He looked down and saw Oliver hurling toward the ground. With his own magic he stopped Oliver's fall, and supported him while they both descended safely to the ground.

It was some minutes before Oliver came back to his senses. He awoke to find himself propped against a large tree. Looking around, he saw the sun was ready to slip below the horizon, Michael was sitting just a few feet away.

"I must have fallen asleep. Where are the others? Come to think of it, where the hell are we?"

"You came up here to help me, remember?" answered Michael.

Oliver stopped to think. "Yeah, I remember. But what did we do?"

"It doesn't matter. It's done, that's all that matters. Let's get back to the others or it'll be dark before we get there."

The others were still in camp when Michael and Oliver returned. Everett and Thomas were calmly sitting on the beach, talking in low tones. Sarah had fallen asleep. She was lying between the two men, with her head on one of the packs.

Thomas jumped up when Michael and Oliver entered the camp. One instant there was no one in the camp but the three of them because of the shield Michael had created for them, and in the next instant, Michael and Oliver appeared, having entered the bubble.

"Don't do that!" he ordered. "You scared the hell out of me."

"Sorry," was Michael's only answer.

"We had better wake Sarah now," he continued. "I think the sooner we move from here the better."

Michael moved across the camp to Sarah to wake her himself. He knelt down beside her and watched for a minute before waking her. She looked so innocent and vulnerable sleeping. In spite of her newly-acquired strength, she was still trusting in Michael and the others to keep her safe from harm.

He rubbed her shoulder and upper arm gently until she woke. She looked up at him with sleepy but smiling eyes. It was too late for Michael to worry about the danger she was in because of him; but he nevertheless wished there had been a way to remove her from jeopardy.

"Where have you been?" she asked as she came awake.

"Just off doing magical stuff with Oliver. Boring stuff really. But now the time has come to make our final plans. So, if you can force that sleep out of your eyes, we'll get down to business."

"I'm ready," she said as she sat up.

"I don't think it's safe to stay here," said Michael once they were altogether. "Even cloaked as we are, I think she could send out those beasts that attacked us at the cabin, and eventually find us. We have to move from here, whether on to the keep or somewhere else doesn't matter, just so long as we move." He turned to Everett. "You said earlier you had a plan to get us in. Now is the time to tell us."

Everett was sitting cross-legged next to Michael; the others were sitting across from him. "Getting in should be easy, as long as we can get up to the hill it sits on unseen. When the first magicians took over the castle with the hopes of starting the enclave, the fear and hate held by non-magicians was at its strongest. Those early magicians were afraid they would be attacked by the others. Sure, they could have defended themselves easily with their magic, but they took vows of non-violence. So rather than possibly being in a position where they would have to fight, they built a bolt-hole."

"You mean like rabbits and other burrowing animals?" asked Thomas.

"Exactly. There is a secret tunnel from the basement of the enclave that leads out through the side of the hill it sits on."

"Wait a minute," interrupted Michael. "I've never heard any-thing about a tunnel."

"Well, of course not," answered Everett. "If you had, it would-n't be a secret tunnel, would it?"

Michael stopped to think about the possibilities of a secret tunnel and why he had not heard of it before. "Well, what's the use of us having a tunnel at the enclave if no one knows it's there?"

"Only teachers were allowed to know of its existence. If we had been able to stay at the enclave, and you had continued your studies, eventually to become a teacher, that would have been one of the rites of passage, to be taught all of the secrets of the enclave."

"Whoa," said Oliver as he leaned forward. "Who cares whether you knew about it before? All that matters is that it's there, and that we can use it. Are you sure you can find the entrance on the hill, Everett? I assume it's hidden."

"Yes, it's hidden. But there will be no trouble finding it. We had to tend to the tunnel as part of our chores as teachers. I've been there before. I can find it."

"Well," offered Sarah, "that takes care of that. If there is a tunnel that Acantha doesn't know about that leads into her keep, and if we have to find a place to hide tonight...what are we waiting for?"

They sat in silence for a short time. Unable to come up with any reasons to question Sarah's logic, the decision was made to start immediately. The packs had not been unloaded, so they quickly secured them over their shoulders and gathered the weapons they had received from Esther.

They were off on the last leg of their journey without stopping to rest, or taking a meal. Only Michael knew that he had survived a battle with Acantha through Oliver, and he realized that Acantha would try to find them now that they were so close.

Rather than making straight to the old castle, they stole south, parallel to the ocean. If Acantha sent her creatures after them, she would send them toward the last spot where they had been before erecting the shield. They had moved up from the beach to an area covered with ice-plant, and short hardy brush, in the hopes of covering their tracks as they moved south.

They were only a half-mile along when they heard the wild baying of the same type of beasts they had struggled with just days earlier. Even shielded from sight as they were, the sound of the unholy din moving down the hillside toward them caused their blood to run cold.

The beasts were still too distant for Michael and the others to see, but by the sound, they were moving fast. "Come on," called Michael as he broke into a run. "We've got to get as far from here as we can."

The others did not waste time with questions. They immediately began running with Michael. The beasts were coming fast down the hill, many times faster than a man could run. They were on a line slightly behind Michael and his friends. Michael had to pace himself to the slowest of the group, Everett, so he could not put on an extra burst of speed to insure that their paths did not converge.

The beasts were easily in sight now. Teeth and razor claws could be seen flashing in the new moon. There were more than a dozen of Acantha's horde racing from the top of the hill.

Sarah felt the chill of fear race down her spine. She trusted in Michael and his power, but the sight of the death-seeking creatures threatened to freeze her heart.

"Behind us," she said as she gasped for breath. "They're going to go behind us. They don't see us."

"They can't see us," answered Everett, also struggling for breath, "but they can smell where we've been."

Looking behind them, Sarah could see the beasts slowing as they put their noses to the ground in hopes of catching the scent of their prey.

Hiding the scent was Michael's only hope of keeping their trail from being found. Without slowing he released a part of his consciousness to mislead the pursuers. Behind them, the sandy soil began an upheaval. Soon sand, dirt, weeds, and bushes were spewing from the ground, ten feet into the air.

Small rocks and dirt pelted the beasts as they charged into the upheaval. Confused and disoriented, the angry creatures began attacking each other. The only foes that were available for venting their frustration and hatred were their own kind.

While behind them the beasts were ripping and tearing at each other, Michael and his friends continued their struggled flight.

"No more," said Everett nearly bent double with exhaustion. "I can't run anymore. Go on without me."

The others all stopped at the same time. Looking back at Everett, they saw that it was true that he could run no further. He was flushed, perspiration coursed in rivulets, making tracks through his dirty face. He had given his all during the journey; but he was too old, and had given too much to have any strength left for a last minute race to safety.

"We're not going on without you, Everett," answered Michael. "Use your mind, not your body. Levitate about a foot off the ground."

"What good is that going to do me? I can float, but I can't fly."

"Maybe you can't fly, but we can pull you. Now, hurry, levitate."

Everett did as Michael instructed. When he was a foot off the ground, Michael took hold of one arm, and Thomas took the other. Turning inland now and heading straight for the dark silhouette of the castle in the distance, Michael and Thomas easily pulled the floating Everett along with them. He looked like a cloth-covered balloon in tow by children as they raced up the hill to Acantha's keep.

Following Everett's direction, they were at the foot of the hill, to the north, when Everett lowered himself to the ground. "It's right around here. There is a rock outcropping with trees growing all.... There, over there!" he said as he pointed to a tree-hidden rock outcropping. "The entrance to the tunnel is hidden behind those rocks."

"Then let's go," said Oliver as he started out ahead of the others.

He was the first to reach the tumble of rocks, and was climbing over and behind them when the others arrived. "I don't see any damn tunnel," he said. "If there was a tunnel, I would have seen it."

Everett moved ahead of the others to where Oliver was standing. "If you got any closer to it, you would fall in. Stand aside." He made a few intricate passes with his hands, ending with a pushing motion with his right hand, and the opening revealed itself.

Oliver stood not five feet from where the opening revealed itself.

"You'd think you have been around magicians long enough to have expected this," said Everett as he disappeared into the black mouth of the tunnel.

Although first to arrive, Oliver was the last to enter the yawning hole in the hillside.

CHAPTER 24

Barely a few feet inside the tunnel, it became pitch black. Although the luminous moon and stars made it easy to see outside, it was not sufficient to push aside the darkness once inside the earth. Michael and Everett provided the necessary light through their magic. Everett carried two small glowing orbs, one in each hand; Michael seemed to radiate with a light of his own, with no apparent effort on his part.

"What about the entrance to the tunnel?" asked Sarah as they began walking.

"That's no problem, dear," replied Everett. "The spell took effect again once we were all inside. If Acantha and her creatures did not know about this place before, they will not find it now."

As they moved further into the depths of the hillside, Sarah felt the massive weight of the earth above them. The walls were not rough-hewn like that of a natural cave, but rather smooth and rounded, about seven feet in height and width. The floor was nearly flat, which made for easy walking.

The cool smoothness of the dark stone, the small diameter of the tunnel, and the blackness ahead of and behind them only intensified Sarah's feeling of fragility. Not wanting to add to the oppressive feeling by walking side by side, with the walls crowding in on them, they spread into a loose line. Everett took the lead, with the others following behind with mouths open in awe.

"We have steps coming up here," remarked Everett. "We go up about one-hundred steps, then the floor levels out for a ways. There will be many more steps later."

"Why aren't there any torches along the walls?" asked Thomas. "It would sure make it easier."

Michael looked around him at the darkness beyond the magical light. "I think that may be the reason there are no torches, Thomas. The magicians that made this tunnel didn't want it to be easy."

"That's exactly right," Everett answered. "The whole purpose of this was an escape route. The magicians could travel through here with their own light, as we are doing. Whoever was pursuing them would have to stop and make torches. The magicians would be out of the tunnel and gone before their enemies got a good start.

"Here are the steps, be careful."

They were soon puffing and panting because of the exertion spent in climbing the steps. They had not rested since flying all day in Oliver's air-boat, and then the mad run from the beach to the foot of the hill.

"I'm glad you got your strength back, Everett," Sarah said, "but I think I need to rest. These steps are about to wear me out."

"We're almost to the top; just a little farther, then we'll rest."

She put her hands on the tops of her knees and pushed, trying to make the climb easier.

\*　　\*　　\*　　\*　　\*

"Damn, where did they go?" Acantha had watched the progress of her wretched creations as they had charged down the hill toward where she had thought Michael was hiding. When she saw the earth exploding around her beasts, she knew the invaders were on the move. Try as she might though, she could not see any sign of them in her crystal bowl.

"They must still be under that spell of concealment." She turned to Croom, who was standing just inside the doorway to her laboratory. "It looks as though you will not get your chance to fulfill my demands tonight. You will stay beside me from now on, until I give you directions otherwise." She looked at the scowling man across the room. "Such anger. Save it for them when they come, do you understand?"

Croom continued to stare at her with malice in his cold dead heart. As they continued to glare at each other, neither speaking, Milo began to make his retreat from the room. He had been too weak to make escape before now, but seeing the beginnings of rebellion from Croom, Milo felt it would be safer if he could somehow escape from the room before Acantha lost her temper.

As Acantha considered the open rebellion from Croom, she caught Milo's movement as he crawled toward the door. Raising her hand and straightening her arm, she gestured to Milo with open palm. He was stopped in his tracks, unable to move further.

"It seems, Croom, as though you have forgotten who is in charge here." She raised her hand and Milo was lifted from the floor. He was now in control of his muscles once again, but suspended from the floor, in mid-air, he was unable to do anything to help himself other than flail about.

The growing terror was reflected in his eyes as Acantha spoke. "You need to be reminded, Croom, of what happens to those that oppose me." She slowly began closing her hand, and Milo expelled a great breath of air, totally clearing his lungs.

With all of the air pushed out of him, he was unable to plead for mercy. His wild thrashing was slowing, and he was beginning to lose consciousness. With a final jerk, Acantha closed her hand into a fist. Milo's tortured body visibly compressed, bones could be heard breaking in the quiet room. Finally blood began spewing from his mouth and nose as his nearly lifeless body began shuddering in shock.

Acantha opened her hand and allowed the empty husk that had been Milo to drop to the floor. "Of course it would be useless to threaten you with death, Croom, since you already have that; but do not forget my power. If you do not wish to walk the earth for eternity, you will stop your useless balking when I give you an order.

"Now, clean up this mess," she said smiling, pointing at what had been Milo, "and get back here as quickly as possible. I need to call my hoard back from the beaches to have them ready when I locate

Michael again." She turned her back on Croom and stalked back to her crystal bowl.

Croom, with a resigned sigh, moved to gather the dead body of Milo. He dragged the limp form down the hall and steps leading to the lower reaches of the castle. Reaching the ground floor, he spotted two of the slaves silently making their way toward the main door.

"Stop!" he ordered.

The two men, startled by the sudden order, stopped and backed against the wall. "Damn," one whispered to the other, "you see, every time we start to make a break for it, that ghoul catches us."

Croom, unaware that the two were attempting an escape, continued, "Take this worthless lump of garbage to the basements and dispose of it." He casually threw the body at the two men, turned on his heel, and left.

"We had better do as he says. He looked like he was in a real bad mood. If he comes down and finds us missing now, we would be in real trouble."

They bent down to roll the body over to get a better hold. "Hey, isn't this that weasel that was always buttering up to the witch?"

"Yeah, that's him. Looks like it don't pay to try to lick her boots, does it?"

"No, I reckon not. Let's get him down to the basements like we're supposed to."

Each grabbed an arm and began dragging Milo's body down the hall, then down to the basements. Upon reaching the bottom floors and disposing of the body, the two slaves lit a candle and sat down on the cold bare floor to think over new plans for escaping from their captivity.

\*      \*      \*      \*      \*

After having rested nearly an hour, Michael and his friends had once again begun moving through the dark narrow tunnel.

"It won't be much further," Everett assured them. "Just one more set of steps, and then another hundred yards or so, and we'll be at the entrance."

"So what are we going to do once we get there?" Thomas asked.

"Then it's up to Michael," Everett replied as he casually pointed over his shoulder at Michael.

Michael continued walking without speaking. With his head tilted down, looking at the floor, he was thinking about the coming battle, wishing things had been different so that he would not be pitted against his sister. Finally, deciding that it was too late to worry about things he could not change, he looked over and smiled at Sarah.

"What will you do when the time comes, Michael?"

"Whatever I am called to do. I'm afraid I won't know what that is until the time arrives."

His answer satisfied no one but they knew he didn't have a better one. They continued their passage through the darkness, climbing the last set of steps, and finally, they came upon a blank wall where the tunnel suddenly stopped.

"This is it," whispered Everett in near reverence. "On the other side of this wall is the basement to Acantha's keep. Perhaps I should begin calling it the Magician's Enclave once again, if we are to wrest it and the ruby away from her."

"How do we get to the other side?" Oliver inquired.

"We just need a little magic is all," Everett replied. "But not just yet, we need to rest before the final battle. Michael will need all the power he can call upon to best Acantha."

After setting down the weapons and supplies that they had brought along with them, they all sank to the rock floor in near exhaustion. Knowing that the ultimate day was at hand, there was very little talk. They all sat quietly, lost in their own private thoughts. It had been a long arduous trek from the Cruz Mountains to where they were now. At least the first part had been, until Oliver, with a stroke of brilliance, had conceived of the flying air-boat.

Thomas was quite pleased with the entire venture, and looked forward with relish to the coming conflict. To him a friendly brawl was a way of celebrating life. What he failed to recognize now, was that this was not to be a friendly brawl. Acantha meant it to be a battle to the death.

Oliver's only concern, as it had been from the very first night when Michael and Sarah surprised him at the door of his shack, was to protect Sarah from harm. He had made his promise to old Gus years before. He meant to fulfill his promise, or die trying.

Michael and Sarah, holding each other, leaning against a wall of the tunnel, silently sharing the thought that perhaps they would be able to return to their old life once this was over; if they survived.

Michael released Sarah from his embrace and slowly climbed to his feet. "I'm going to go back down the tunnel a little way and prepare myself by meditating. You'll be all right here till I get back."

Sarah replied, "Oh...I had hoped we would be able to spend this bit of time together! I mean, we don't know what is going to happen when we break through into the keep."

"Yes, and that is why I need go off by myself for a while. I want to end this as much as you do, but if we are to be successful I must be as prepared as possible."

He leaned down to give Sarah a tender kiss. "I know that, Michael," she said. "I was just being selfish. It's not such a bad thing to be a little selfish at a time like this."

She stood and gave him a gentle push back in the direction from which they had come. "Go now. Prepare yourself. I will be waiting here for you when you return."

He smiled at her and gave her pale face a gentle caress. "I won't be long."

Turning to leave he spoke to Everett. "I'll be back shortly, Everett."

"What?" Everett replied with a start. He was lost in his own private thoughts and had not heard what had been exchanged between Michael and Sarah. "What?" he repeated.

"I said I will return shortly. I am going to meditate for a bit before we attack Acantha's stronghold."

"Attack? Yes, that's what we'll be doing, I suppose. It would do you well to prepare yourself. We will all get some much needed rest while you are gone."

He waved Michael away and once again became lost in his own thoughts about how this evil had come into the world, and the integral part that he had played in its coming.

When Michael reached a part of the tunnel where he felt that he was completely alone, he sat down on the floor and extinguished the globe of light that he had produced to guide him. It was very easy for him now to slip into the trance, and out of his body. He meant to make one final trip to Acantha's side before they attempted to regain the ruby.

Moving with his mind's eye alone, he traveled back through the tunnel, past where his friends sat in silence, waiting for the time to do battle. He moved up to and then through the wall at the end of the tunnel, seeing and understanding the magic that it would take to open the secret door into the castle. He saw the two men sitting on the hard stone floor of the basement. Michael idly noticed them as he passed, vaguely remembering them as the two men he had seen on his last trip, then gave them no further thought.

Rather than cutting through walls, floors, or closed doors, he took the route he would have to take by foot. He wanted to see who or what may be around to stop him from reaching Acantha. He was surprised to see the stairs and hallways leading up from the basements and into the upper reaches of the old castle deserted. Perhaps Acantha did not realize how close they were to achieving their goal. Perhaps she was able to overcome the evil of the ruby, and was even now waiting for Michael's help.

"Maybe more than I should expect," thought Michael ruefully. It was obvious that she had lost track of them because of Michael's cloaking spell, and believed that they were still outside in the open. Her defenses would be outside, on the grounds of her keep, watching all of the known entrances.

He was nearly to the top of the tower and still did not see any defenses. He couldn't understand why there was nothing up here to stop them from an attack. Surely Acantha was at least concerned enough about the threat from Michael that she would have some protection by her side.

When he entered her laboratory he finally saw Acantha's protector. Croom was standing morosely, just inside the door, glaring at Acantha's back. Michael stopped in surprise, it had been so long since he had seen Croom that he had failed to consider him as a problem. If he was to meet Croom away from Acantha, he felt that he now had enough power to destroy him. But if he had to contend with Acantha and Croom at the same time, he wasn't sure.

As Michael paused, Acantha turned toward him. "Michael, how nice of you to visit me," she said sarcastically. "Croom, aren't you going to speak to our guest?"

Croom looked about the room, searching for Michael, knowing for sure that Acantha had finally gone totally insane. The room was empty except for the two of them, and the assorted vile paraphernalia that she needed to work her black magic.

"If you're here to try one final time to dissuade me from destroying you and your friends," she spat, "you can forget it! You are wasting time for both of us."

"Then you would rather that we do battle?"

"No Michael, I would rather that you and your stinking friends do me the service of coming out of hiding, and then dying on the spot. Then I could take what belongs to me without all of this trouble."

Michael flinched from her scornful words, but continued to attempt reason. "I have nothing that belongs to you, Acantha. Neither the emerald nor the ruby belongs to either of us."

Acantha gave a sharp bark of derisive laughter. "You're wrong, brother. These rings were given to me, they are mine to control."

"Given to you?" Michael recoiled in disbelief. "They weren't given to you, you stole them!"

"Not so, brother," she answered. She could sense Michael's discomfort, and relished in it. "Our foolish teachers kept the key to the box that held the stones safe. I could not have gotten it. Someone else used the key and took the stones, then gave them to me."

"Don't be foolish," snapped Michael. "Who would do such a thing?"

"Think about it, Michael. I didn't understand at the time why they were given to me. But later when Everett told you only those of our bloodline could use it, I understood."

"You were watching us even then!" exclaimed Michael.

"Of course I was! That's trivial. Think about what I just told you. Who knew the stones could only be used by our bloodline?"

Michael thought for a moment before answering. "I don't know, our parents I suppose...Everett obviously."

Acantha threw her arms out to her sides with palms up, as though she were bestowing a great truth upon him.

"Now, there is some knowledge for you to deal with! Go away now, I have work to do." She abruptly turned her back on Michael, acting as though she was no longer aware of his presence. Croom continued to look at her as though she had lost her mind.

"What are you playing at, Acantha?" demanded Michael. "Do you really expect me to believe that Everett gave you the stones to use?"

Acantha spun back around to face Michael. Pointing a threatening finger at where she sensed him to be, she answered, "I don't care what you believe! Everett wanted power. He thought he could get it through me." She made a dismissive gesture with her hand. "What do I care if you are too stupid to believe me? Ask him. See if he has the courage to tell you the truth. You have power now, you can sense if he lies to you."

Michael was furious with the implication that his old friend would have done something such as this. He began to move away from the room. He left one final thought with Acantha as he left. "You will regret telling me this lie. I finally see there is no other way to stop you...and I will stop you!"

As he fled the room, he could hear Acantha's insane laughter chasing him down the hall.

CHAPTER 25

It took Michael just a moment to return to his body. He was seething with anger. He did not know where to direct his anger yet. If Acantha had lied to him, his anger would be well directed at her, but if she was telling the truth, what did that mean? Everett had tried repeatedly to get Michael to help him recover the ruby. Was it just because he wanted both of the stones together; and with someone he could control? Or was he truly concerned about the damage the two stones could cause in the wrong hands?

There was only one way Michael would ever know the truth. He would have to question Everett, and not be swayed by friendship when considering the answers. Gathering his resolve, Michael climbed to his feet. He sent his thoughts to Everett. They entered Everett's mind much in the way Acantha's thoughts had entered Croom's; but without the feeling of rape that was present with Acantha's probing.

"Everett, can you hear me?"

Everett jumped from the alien invasion. He looked around at the others to see if they had heard the voice in his head. The other three showed no response, and did not stir from their resting spots.

"Michael, is that you?" Everett answered within his own mind.

"Yes. Come to where I am meditating, Everett."

"Why, Michael. What's wrong?"

"We will discuss that when we are face to face. I will wait here for you."

Everett took one last look at his fellow travelers to insure they were still resting quietly. They had not moved since before his strange conversation with Michael. Everett rose quietly to his feet and began the short walk down the tunnel to Michael.

He carried two globes of light, one in each hand. In a very short time, Everett saw Michael outlined by the far reaches of the glow. He was still sitting on the floor, as though meditating. Everett walked up to him and sat beside him without saying a word.

A couple of minutes passed before Michael stirred and recognized Everett's presence. He turned to the old magician and looked deeply into his eyes for some time before speaking.

"I have been up to Acantha's laboratory. She said some disturbing things."

"Everything she has said or done for the last number of months have been disturbing," replied Everett.

"Yes, well – this was one of the worst." Michael leaned forward to get closer to his old friend. "She says that you took the talismans. She says that you gave them to her."

Everett said nothing. He just sat in the near darkness, staring into the gloom.

"Well, did you?" Michael inquired.

"It's not the way you make it sound." He got up and began to pace in front of Michael. "There were two beliefs at the enclave. One was that the talismans should be kept under lock and key. The other was that the stones could be used for the greater benefit of society. That we could help to bring the people up from fear and superstition, and approach the high level of life that our ancestors knew."

"Well, it has become evident which course was correct, hasn't it?" spat Michael, his irritation finally getting the better of him.

Everett threw his arms in the air in a helpless gesture. "I still believe we were right. Yes, it went badly, but that was because the stones were given to the wrong person. We had only you or your sister to choose from. You didn't seem to take magic seriously, so we chose your sister." Everett stopped his pacing and turned to Michael, "We should have chosen you."

"How dare you think you could have chosen either of us without telling us what you were up to!" exploded Michael. "Did you tell Acantha the dangers of the stones, did you tell her the trouble it could cause, and did you tell her of the evil history of the stones?"

"We thought we were right!"

"Well, you weren't!" returned Michael in anger as he stood.

"Perhaps, as I said, we chose the wrong sibling. But now we have a chance to put things right! When you regain the ruby you can lead the people to a higher level!"

"My God, man, wake up!" shouted Michael in his fury. "If...and I repeat if...I can regain the ruby, I'll either lock them up for eternity, or drop them in the deepest part of the ocean!"

As Michael started back toward the others, Everett reached out, grasping his shirt to halt his progress. "Don't you see the good that we could do with both of the stones in concert?"

Michael whirled on the old magician. "All I see is the great harm that just one of these stones has caused. No...if I succeed I will do my best to see to it that they never see the light of day again!" He paused and then continued, "I don't know that I can trust you anymore. You have caused great destruction, hidden the truth from me, and even lied straight out. Even now I do not know whether you are working for what is best, or just for what you want."

Everett straightened his short pudgy frame as much as possible, showing what pride he could. "I am working for the betterment of the people as a whole."

"And you are the only one to decide how that should be thrust upon them?"

"I am doing what no other is in a position to do!" replied Everett testily.

"That is not a decision for you to make." Michael expelled a deep sigh. "I will be going to Acantha's laboratory alone. We will stay together until then, in case we need to fight our way there. When this is over..."

Michael turned on his heel and strode up to where his friends waited. Everett visibly shrunk in upon himself when he heard Michael words of damnation. He stood for some time with head bowed in sorrow before he slowly made his way back. By the time Everett returned to the end of the tunnel where the others were, they were already on their feet, having been roused by Michael.

He said nothing as he watched them prepare for battle. They would be needing little now, only the axes for Oliver and Thomas, and the pitchfork for Sarah. Michael and Everett would carry no weapons.

As Michael quietly strode to the wall at the end of the tunnel, Thomas gave Everett a curious glance. He was obviously aware that something was wrong. Everett consciously pulled up his slouched shoulders, and forced a confident smile. He would have to act as though everything was as it should be if his friends were to be successful. The last thing they needed at this point was them to be aware of a rift between him and Michael.

Everett still wanted Michael to regain the ruby, no matter what happened to it in the future. His original intentions in giving the stones to Acantha had been good. He honestly believed that he and his supporters would be able to guide the people of the world back to the glory that their ancestors had known before the Magicians' War. But now that all of his good intentions had come crashing down around him, he was only too aware that the ruby could no longer be allowed to be controlled by Acantha.

Michael had his eyes closed and was making strange passes with his hands. Before the others could understand what he was doing, the great wall in front of them began to move to the side with a loud rumbling and groaning noise. The stone floor they stood on seemed to vibrate and shake with the movement of the wall.

When the wall had moved completely to the side, the travelers looked into a large room in the basement of the old castle. All but Michael were surprised to see two men, mouths open and huddled together, staring back at them. Thomas and Oliver made ready with their axes, expecting the two men to charge at them once their surprise was past.

"No! No!" one of the two men protested when they saw the axes brought to the ready. "We have no quarrel with you!" Raising his hands in a forestalling motion, he hastily continued, "The sorceress of this place stole us from our home in the woods. If you have come to do battle with her, we assure you that we will not try to stop you."

"A fat lotta good it would do you to try to stop us." replied Thomas as he stood over the two.

"Wait!" said Michael hastily. Speaking to the two men, he added, "You said you were taken from your home in the woods, are you the husband of Esther, and Brian's father?"

"Yes!" answered one of the men. Standing quickly he continued, "Have you seen them? Are they all right?"

"Yes. In fact we just left them a couple of days ago. They are quite anxious to see you safely home."

The other man jumped to his feet, clasping the first by the shoulders. "Did you hear that, Marcus? We're going to get out of here!"

Michael pointed behind him at the still open doorway into the tunnel. "Just go into that tunnel, it will lead you to the outside, near the bottom of this hill. You'll need to take your candle with you."

"What about you?" asked Marcus as his brother went for the candle.

"We'll be staying behind. We have a score to settle with Acantha."

Marcus' brother was at the opening of the tunnel now, motioning him to hurry and join him.

"Do you have a chance of beating her?" Marcus asked with real concern in his voice.

"I believe so," answered Michael. "At least we're going to give it our best try."

"What are you waiting for, Marcus?" his brother asked. "We have our freedom given to us, let's take it before it's too late."

Marcus turned to answer his brother's plea. "If these people are not successful, then the witch will just pull us back, and it will be harder for us since we tried to escape. No, I'm going to stay and give what help I can. If we are to be truly free, we need to be safe from the threat of being pulled back."

The second man groaned and walked back to Marcus. "We don't even have any weapons, what good are we going to be in a fight?"

"There's plenty of wood down here we can use as clubs. We'll make do."

All conversation stopped as from the upper reaches of the castle they could hear the wild frantic baying of Acantha's beasts. As they listened, they could hear the awful sound coming closer.

"I believe it is too late for decisions, woodsmen," said Everett. "Acantha has sensed our presence and set her beasts upon us. Grab anything available for use as a weapon and prepare to do battle."

Michael and his friends stood and listened to the sounds coming ever closer as Marcus and his brother scrabbled for the strongest pieces of wood they could find in the rubble of the basement room.

"What happened to your spell of concealment, Michael?" asked Sarah. "She could not locate us before, why now?"

"I don't know. Perhaps she has her own spells already in place here to counteract mine. But no matter, the time is at hand. Everett, come to the front. We will use our magic as the first line of defense. If we are lucky, none will pass us and the others will not need to face those razor claws."

Marcus and his brother turned to the tunnel as they heard the strange baying echoing up from the depths. "I think our escape has been cut off. She has sent those beasts you spoke of through the tunnel."

"I thought she didn't know about the tunnel," said Oliver as he looked from the stairs leading up to the main floors over to the tunnel entrance.

"She must have seen us come out on this side, and traced it back.

"No more talk, here they come!"

Down the narrow stairs rushed the charging hoard of Acantha's beasts. Blood-red hairless skin bulged and pulsated in the scant candlelight. Their evil eyes glinted with hate and rage as they fought one another to be the first down the stairs. Tumbling over one another in their haste, they soon reached the bottom of the stairs, some thirty feet from Michael and his friends.

Immediately Michael and Everett lashed out with their magic, and the beasts were exploding in great blobs of flesh and blood before they could mount a charge. Michael and Everett would have been able to destroy all of the beasts if that had been the only point of attack. But as the numbers that were spilling down the stairwell began to diminish, the beasts that were traveling through the tunnel reached the entrance to the basements.

"Here they come!" yelled Marcus as he swung his club, bringing down the first beast coming through the door.

Almost immediately all of the defenders were swinging ax or club, with Sarah stabbing with her pitch-fork to keep the beasts from rending her apart.

"Everett," called Michael, "see if you can get that door closed with your magic! I'm going up the stairs to Acantha. If I can stop her, these abhorrent creatures will disappear."

Without waiting for response, Michael raced for the stairs leading up to Acantha's tower laboratory. Slipping and sliding in the spilled blood of the beasts, Michael reached the steps and began running up as quickly as possible.

The sound of the raging battle was soon lost to him, and he could only hope that his friends would be as lucky as they were valiant.

It took only a couple of minutes to reach the upper floors, but he was frightfully aware that a couple of minutes may be more than his friends could hold out against the invading hoard.

He was still running at full speed when he reached the door to Acantha's laboratory. Without slowing, he threw a ball of green lightning, shattering the door into splinters. Rushing into the room, he saw Acantha, casually standing by her beautiful crystal bowl. Next to her was Croom, standing with no expression on his face, but eyes boring into Michael.

"Well, Michael," she said slowly, "it's been quite some time since I have seen you in the flesh. It seems you have not heeded my warnings."

"I have no time to talk, or to reason with you Acantha. Stop your attack in the basements and give over the ruby."

"And if not?"

"Then I will be forced to destroy you, and take the ruby by force!"

Acantha raised her head back and howled with laughter. In an instant she stopped laughing, and jerked her head down to glare at Michael. Throwing her hands up, she unleashed a lightning bolt of fiery red.

Michael barely had time to erect a shield and dodge to the side. The bolt of lightning seared into his shield, then bounced off and sizzled harmlessly into the wall.

Quickly recovering, Michael raised his hands and threw his own emerald bolt of magic at Acantha. Over the past few weeks of Michael's travels, Acantha had been doing all of the attacking, and had never been attacked herself. She was momentarily surprised by the strength and rage of Michael's magic, and was seared on her left shoulder before she was able to erect her own shield.

They stood facing each other from opposite sides of the room now, both encased in their magical bubbles; Michael's green, Acantha's red. Glaring at each other, they began the attack anew. Soon the room was ablaze with the blinding light of their magic. Chairs and tables were overturned; paper, ancient tapestries, and other lightweight objects flew through the air as the powers roiled and lashed through the room.

Both of their shields had started out as pristine green and red bubbles, now both of them were shot through with cracks of the opposing color. It was now a race to see which magician would tire first, and weaken to the point that they would no longer be able to keep their shield erected.

"Now! Damn you, Croom. Now!" shrieked Acantha.

Croom immediately raced across the room and began clawing at the cracks in Michael's shield. Michael was afraid that if he diverted any power from his attack on Acantha to deal with Croom, his lapse would give her the upper hand and he would be destroyed. Yet he could not ignore Croom, for if he did, the maniacal man would succeed in tearing Michael's weakened shield apart.

As he was worrying about what to do, Croom flew from the shield in front of him to crash headlong against the far wall. Through the maelstrom in the room charged Everett. The thin wisps of white hair on his head stood on end, and the brown robe swirled violently about him, showing his pale spindly legs.

In an instant he was upon the injured Croom, sending the full force of his magic into the dead man. Acantha saw what was happening and realized that if the old man managed to destroy Croom, she would have to deal with both of the magicians.

She momentarily diverted some of her power, throwing a bolt at the old magician now grappling on the floor with Croom. Everett arched his back in a spasm from the pain as the bolt of power reached him.

Seeing this, Michael went deep into himself for all the power that he could gain from the fully-awakened emerald. The room blazed with green light, momentarily blinding even Michael. When he was finally able to see again, he saw Acantha still standing, staring at him from across the room. But the room was still. The paper and tapestries that were flying around the room were now slowly fluttering to the floor.

On second look, he could see that Acantha was not moving and the red shield that she had erected had changed to a hazy green, surrounding her like an aura. The aura extended from Acantha, down her arm and across to encompass Everett and Croom, where they were locked in unmoving battle.

After a couple of minutes of watching, and seeing no movement from either of the three, Michael slowly let his defensive shield down. He walked through the clutter of the room until he reached the still, aura- enshrouded form of Acantha. He felt the emerald green haze surrounding her and was surprised to find it hard and unyielding. He moved over to kneel where Everett and Croom were locked in battle, and felt that the enveloping haze was just the same there.

He looked at the pain frozen on the face of the old magician and felt remorse for all that he had said when he had learned how Acantha had gained control of the ruby. "Oh, old man. What has become of you?" he asked while tears freely tracked down his cheeks.

The three people were trapped in a state of stasis created by Michael's unfettered spell. He could not know how long the spell would last, but he was sure it would not decay anytime soon. Acantha, Croom, and Everett would remain gripped in this moment of battle while time passed unnoticed around them.

Gathering his courage, Michael rose and left the laboratory. Once he was away from the scene of the battle, he remembered the danger that the others had been in when he left, and hurried down the stairs to the basements once again.

Reaching the basement, he found his friends huddled around a fallen body by the now closed doorway into the tunnel. The mangled bodies of the beasts were lying around them. Some were completely unmarked; all were unmoving. They had died when Acantha had become trapped in stasis.

"What happened here?" asked Michael as he rushed to the group.

Sarah looked up with tears in her eyes. "It's Big Thomas. He was laying waste to these beasts when one of them got inside his swinging axe. Thomas fell with chest and stomach slashed open. Just then all of the beasts just fell down dead." She looked back down at Thomas who was lying near death.

"We're going to lose him, Michael," said Oliver from where he knelt by Thomas' head.

"No! I won't allow it!" raged Michael. "There has been too much death already." Michael fell to his knees, and then lay across Thomas' body, covering it as near as possible with his own. Both men were instantly covered by the shimmering green light that Michael had released earlier in Acantha's laboratory. The light was so bright, the others were forced to turn their heads in pain.

When the light finally died down, they turned back to see where Thomas was lying. Michael was just pulling himself from the big man, and they could see that Thomas' wounds had healed. In fact the big man was beginning to groan and regain consciousness.

"What the hell happened?" he asked as he rose to a sitting position.

"Oh, Thomas!" cried Sarah as she rushed to him.

After a brief hug, Thomas lurched to his feet. "Well, we had best get to battling this witch sister of yours! It looks like we're done down here."

Michael chuckled at Thomas sudden zest. The mountain man seemed to not realize that moments ago he had been near death.

"Relax, Thomas," he said. "All of you, our quest has come to an end. Although not dead, Acantha is no longer able to do harm. Walk with me up to her laboratory and I will tell you of the battle that you slept through."

Although puzzlement was evident on his face, Thomas and the others followed Michael up the stairs and listened while he told of the battle with Acantha.

EPILOGUE

When the dawn finally arrived, Michael and Sarah were standing by the low wall surrounding the gardens outside the castle. The peacefulness of the morning belied the violence of the previous night. The early morning birds in the gardens sang their salute to the rising sun. The very air was crystalline in its purity. They stood with hands linked, looking out over the landscape that descended to the ocean, as it brightened with each passing moment of the sun's ascension.

Michael had made the decision to stay and reopen the magician's enclave. Since he could not get past the aura surrounding Acantha to retrieve the ruby ring, he felt it was necessary to train future magicians should the spell decay after his days. Never again would he allow the cursed power of the ruby to be loosed on the people.

Sarah would not leave Michael's side and swore to stay with him to help insure the success of the new enclave. Thomas and Oliver also wished to stay with their new friends.

Marcus and his brother made a hasty return to their home in the woods. Marcus made the promise to ask his son, Brian, if he would honor the enclave by becoming its first student.

"What about Everett, Michael?" asked Sarah as she looked over the beauty of the coast. "I mean, the pain that shows in his face, will he feel that through the years until the spell wears off?"

"No, I don't think so. I think that for them, the time from when I set the spell until it finally decays years from now, will seem like an instant to them. I only hope I will have magicians that are ready and strong enough to deal with Acantha when that time finally comes."

"With what you can teach them, and your friends to help you," Sarah said, "Acantha doesn't stand a chance."

"The only support I need is you," replied Michael as he bent to kiss her.

They embraced briefly before they turned to walk back into the new magician's enclave.

\*　　　\*　　　\*　　　\*　　　\*

Stay current with the thrilling stories of "The Enchanted Stones" series from the brilliant pen of Donald Craghead. Make sure to visit the TheEnchantedEmerald.com online, and put your name on the list to be notified when the next book is released.

## Other books from Seton Publishing

Mokki's Peak - Tony Seton

Silent Alarm - Tony Seton

Deki-san - Tony Seton

Equinox - Tony Seton

No Soap, Radio - Tony Seton

Paradise Pond - Tony Seton

Selected Writings - Tony Seton

The Brink - Tony Seton

Jennifer - Tony Seton

The Francie LeVillard Mysteries - Vol I-IX - Tony Seton

Trinidad Head - Tony Seton

Dead as a Doorbell - Tony Seton

Just Imagine - Tony Seton

Musings on Sherlock Holmes - Tony Seton

The Autobiography of John Dough, Gigolo - Tony Seton

Silver Lining - Tony Seton

Mayhem - Tony Seton

The Omega Crystal - Tony Seton

Truth Be Told - Tony Seton

The Quality Interview / Getting it Right
    on Both Sides of the Mic - Tony Seton

From Terror to Triumph /
    The Herma Smith Curtis Story - Tony Seton

Don't Mess with the Press / How to Write, Produce, and
    Report Quality Television News - Tony Seton

Right Car, Right Price - Tony Seton

The Dedicated Life of an American Soldier - Ray Ramos

Life Is a Bumpy Road - Tony Albano

From Hell to Hail Mary / A Cop's Story - Frank DiPaola

From Colored Town to Pebble Beach /
    The Story of the Singing Sheriff - Pat DuVal

The Early Troubles - Gerard Rose

The Boy Captain - Gerard Rose

Bless Me Father - Gerard Rose

For I Have Sinned - Gerard Rose

A Western Hero - Gerard Rose

Red Smith in LA Noir  - David Jones

The Shadow Candidate - Rich Robinson

Hustle is Heaven - Duncan Matteson

Vision for a Healthy California - Bill Monning

Three Lives of a Warrior - Phil Butler

Live Better Longer - Hugh Wilson

Green-Lighting Your Future / How You Can
Manifest the Perfect Life - John Koeberer